EYE OF A NEEDLE:

And other stories

EYE OF A NEEDLE:

And other stories

Cornelia Fick

Published by Feathers Publications, First edition, 2016
PO Box 314 Maraisburg
1700
South Africa

ISBN: 062072319X
ISBN-13:9780620723190

Cover by Caligraphics
Designed and printed by CreateSpace

To my father who also wanted to write.

TABLE OF CONTENTS

ACKNOWLEDGEMENTS

The following stories were originally published in the following magazines and anthologies: 'Last will', *Botsotso 17*; 'The list' and 'Home sweet home', *Itch, The Creative Journal*; 'To die for', *Ladybox Books*; 'Home sweet home', 'Getting along', 'Coffee', 'Knit one', 'An epitaph', *Tyhini 2015;* 'Flying ants', 'Courage the mouse', 'Stolen', *Tyhini 2014*. Thanks to Eben Venter, my supervisor, Ruth Longhurst and Tina Williams, my editors, P Fick for the idea of a walking school and Rian Malan for his input in the story 'DD goes to hospital'.

Information in the story, 'Flying ants', was compiled from different encyclopaedias, mainly The World Book Encyclopaedia (1993), World Book Inc., London. 'Begoogled' uses entries from Wikipedia. 'Takotsubo cardiomyopathy', accessed online, 2016.

Information in 'To die for' about the wheel of control is from the Duluth model. Structure and headings of 'Care plan' was derived from *The Nursing Process* (UK), a legal document.

If you want to awaken all of humanity, then awaken all of yourself. If you want to eliminate the suffering in the world, then eliminate all that is dark and negative in yourself. Truly, the greatest gift you have to give is that of your own self-transformation. Lao Tzu

If you do not change direction, you may end up where you are heading. Lao Tzu

THE BEGGAR

Hi. I'm a homeless writer. I stand at the corner of William Nicol Drive and Sloane Street in Bryanston, South Africa. How did I get here? Well, that's a long story. I had big dreams while growing up; I wanted to be an architect, maybe even a doctor. But that's kinda difficult without money, or parents.

I wear a girl's tartan coat, frayed at the edges. If you see me I'm always bare feet. My big feet hang from my spindly legs in khaki shorts. They have hard calluses for outdoor walking.

My home is under a bridge. I can't tell you where, because you will want to call the police to report it, and then they will come and tear it down.

Don't feel sorry for me. On a good day I make close to R200, which I spend on food, cold-drink and provisions for our survival. Provisions, that's a big word, a word you wouldn't expect me to use when you drive by in your fancy car. But there is a lot about me you don't know.

I don't speak when I beg. I just bring my hand to my mouth in a repetitive motion to show I need food. Some things can be said without words. I hide my accent (I went to a Model C school), but also once you speak you leave yourself open to a reply.

I carry a plastic bag for drivers to place their rubbish in; a walking dustbin.

My stories are about what I have seen. I detest people who write themselves into a story all the time as if they are the most important thing in the world. You aren't, you know?

I make up stories about the people I meet every day. You'd be surprised at what you can observe standing at a robot. People-watching is my favourite pastime. How many people do what they love each day?

I only work during peak hours; in the morning when people go to work and in the evening when they come home. That is my busy period. Every other time is a waste of energy; irritable housewives shouting at fidgety children, cheating husbands with their secretaries, surly teenagers. Besides, there is something in the frank stare of a child that makes me uncomfortable, even ashamed, to stand here: a man who doesn't work.

I became tired of looking for work. Trying and being disappointed. There are a lot of young people like me on the streets. Some turned to crime; I turned to begging. That happens when you don't finish school, but also when you do.

You see people with degrees here. They are the sad-looking ones, trying to advertise their learning on a cardboard poster. Initially they brag about their education – this course at that university, distinctions – then after a while their placard just says 'Looking for work, any work'. Then they progress to silent begging, like me. It's hilarious.

Friends are hard to come by. I saw it written on the back window of a minibus taxi: 'When days are dark, friends are few'. My only friend is a rat that comes to the dustbin on the corner to root through the trash. He doesn't know he is my friend, dumb thing. Sometimes I call to him and he scurries away.

"Hello, Irvin."

Who's that? Don't look. Don't look. Obviously, it's someone who knows me.

"Irvin? You remember me?"

No, I don't remember anything about my past life, and less about my future life. It's too—

"We were together at varsity."

Oh shit, I have to get out of here.

"You did so well at school. What happened to you? Why are you here?"

Damn. She's going to cry. That's all I need, false people blubbering.

"Your parents are looking for you. Hey, where are you running to? Irvin!"

Who does she think she is, giving herself the right to speak to me? My parents… I'm not interested. And don't you dare think that I'll tell you everything about me. I've learned not to trust.

You see the underbelly of society when you beg for a living. Some people are just angry for no reason. Some are polite, while others are plain dodgy. They invite you into their cars and you think that they're gonna be nice…

They think I'm odd. Usually I steal their pens and paper. Once, I copied something from the encyclopaedia. But mostly my head is my notebook. The writing beggar, that's what they call me.

Here's a challenge for you. They say people tell their lives through their stories. See if you can find mine. Heh-heh-heh. After that, you can help me find my parents, and my dreadlocks. Someone stole them.

I once had a friend for twenty-four hours, a young woman who was sitting next to the road. She was afraid, hiding from someone. I took her in, looked after her. The next morning she left without saying goodbye. That's people for you: rude, grasping.

At the end of the day, around nine in the evening, you'll find me sitting under a floodlight on the bridge, reading the newspaper. Next to me will be my housemate, with his blanket around him. Usually he is swaying, a flower in a breeze, or one of those L-shaped robots with arms stretched across the road, shaking in the wind. The survival provisions are for him; a plastic bottle and glue. He sucks on it, a baby who can't get enough. Without this milk he doesn't know how to be in the world.

I can't face the world alone.

He isn't really my friend, sometimes he steals from me. But no relationship is perfect.

FLYING ANTS

After their brief mating flight, the king and queen land on the ground and shed their wings. They search for a suitable home with access to cellulose, burrow underground and seal their chamber to start a family. The queen initially lays about two dozen eggs, which hatch in two weeks. The king stays with the queen and mates with her for life.

Although it is almost noon, Mrs Prinn is dressed in an old blue gown that flaps open from where it is anchored by one button on her chest. The other buttons have fallen off long ago. From under her gown, when she moves, peeps a short nightdress revealing dimply legs in knee-high stockings and furry boot-slippers with soles worn thin on the heels and the instep of her right foot.

It's Friday, and she is sitting on the couch, her hands around a tall mug of Rooibos. She inhales the bush tea that grows wild on the slopes of the Cederberg mountains, and takes a sip. It's perfect, just as she likes it, with lots of milk and three teaspoons of sugar. She picks up the remote control of the television set, increases the volume. Big Brother Africa, her beloved show, fills the room.

Blowing on the hot tea, she sips delicately. She reaches out and strokes the jagged tear in the striped material of the couch where her son, Mason, had plunged his pocket knife. He had been ten at the time; angry because she had forgotten to polish his shoes.

He is thirteen now and still angry, the only difference being his spotty skin and deepening voice. Mrs Prinn tugs at the fraying edges of the tear, smoothing it to look less like a gaping mouth.

She has just finished tidying the kitchen, clearing away the breakfast bowls and cereals that each member of the family likes: bran flakes for her husband, John, who tends towards constipation; diet cereal for her daughter, Jessie; and sugar-coated rice for Mason. She doesn't have a pet cereal; she eats whatever is left over when someone declares theirs stale and opens a new box.

On Big Brother Africa the inmates are eating breakfast. Mrs Prinn notices that they do not all eat together but in little groups, displaying the alliances they have formed during their stay in the Big Brother house.

It's the same in her family. Jessie, a lithesome sixteen-year-old, and John eat breakfast together after getting dressed for school and work. Jessie wears grey trousers with her blue blazer. John, well, he wears whatever Jessie decides on.

Mrs Prinn listens to them as she lies in bed: "Not that tie, Daddy," followed by giggles. "Where's your sense of fashion?"

He laughs gently as he loosens his tie, inviting her into his wardrobe to choose for him. Inevitably, it isn't what Mrs Prinn would've chosen, but he never asks for her opinion and she's too timid to volunteer.

Her work doesn't require her to get dressed.

They get on well, Jessie and her father. This may be why, when they go on their annual holiday to the beach in Durban and have to decide on a restaurant, John takes no note of Mrs Prinn's soft-spoken suggestions of this place or that place. Instead, he leans forward and asks Jessie, "What would you like to eat, my dear?"

Mrs Prinn then echoes Jessie's suggestions. They probably sound like the call and answer of an African drum, she thinks wryly. Boom: "Let's eat Chinese." Bam: "Chinese is nice." Boom: "No–no. What about some pizza?" Bam: "Your father likes pizza." They make a good team, she and Jessie, playing their drum, eager to please the man in their life.

Absent-mindedly she fingers the last button on her gown. Listen to the show. What's wrong with you today? It doesn't help to think too much. Just endure. Thinking brings an ache that can paralyse her for days, weeks, sometimes for months. Listen to Big Brother. They are forming new alliances. Who is whose love interest?

I wonder what it feels like to have your life in the spotlight all the time. The thought just pops into her head. No place to hide. Mrs Prinn sighs again and goes to her bedroom. She doesn't bother to take off her gown, gets into bed and pulls the duvet over her head. Today is one of those days when she won't get anything done.

The king mates repeatedly with the queen and she develops extra ovaries to lay more eggs. She may lay between 20 000 – 30 000 eggs at a time. The ovaries distend her abdomen, increasing her size and making it more difficult to move.

He has just finished a late breakfast. Looking up, he sees his wife sweeping. He drops his gaze to hide his disapproval but it wells up in his chest, causing him to frown and pull down the edges of his thin lips.

There is something wrong with her skirt. It doesn't seem to fit properly; it hangs longer in front than at the back. He tries to think of a reason. Is it because she leans forward when she walks to accommodate her big behind or is her bum hitching the skirt up at the back? He cannot tell. All he knows is that her skirt reveals the back of her knees.

Her buttocks jiggle as she sweeps, they juggle as she walks. Up, down, up, down. Other women's may sway sideways, but hers goes up and down, singing a rhythmic song; one for you and one for me. She is obese. A man could sit on those buttocks and hitch a ride. He is glad that his daughter doesn't take after her mother. She probably has the good genes of his side of the family.

Can anyone blame him for not asking his wife to accompany him to functions at his school anymore? What will the staff say about him, their principal? And she is boring; her conversations centre around what's currently happening on Big Brother Africa. Fortunately, his daughter has slipped effortlessly into the role of being his companion to awards and school dances. With her on his arm, he feels young, attractive and rejuvenated.

Sometimes when they walk together as a family, he finds himself reaching for his daughter's hand. It makes up for the burden of having to walk next to the waddle of his wife.

The king and queen feed the first offspring. After that, these offspring take care of the nest. The queen secretes special chemicals to differentiate them. Some develop enlarged heads with big jaws; these are the soldiers that protect the nest. They cannot feed themselves. When threatened, they bang their heads together. Some become workers; they build protective tunnels to search for food, extend the nest and feed the young nymphs, the queen and the soldiers.

Mrs Prinn is washing the breakfast dishes in the kitchen sink. She ducks as Mason sprays her with his water gun, shrieking with laughter. She holds up a hand to protect her face. If she endures silently he will soon tire of the game. Mason empties his gun and goes to the bathroom for a refill.

John enters. He sits down at the table with a pen and paper to draw up the shopping list. "What do we need?" he says.

They do not attend church anymore. John left their traditional Anglican church to join a charismatic church so that he could become a pastor. He showed the way in prayer, lifting up his hands and speaking in tongues. His association with this church had ended, however, when he quarrelled with the founder over an appropriate salary for such a talented preacher as himself. "Are you deaf?"

"I'm thinking."

"Will you hurry up then?"

Mrs Prinn would love to go back to her old church where she was the treasurer of the Mother's Union. But she is philosophical about her sacrifice. Such is the course of a woman's life once she mates. He leads and she follows. It is the natural order of things.

"We need washing powder," Mrs Prinn says tentatively.

"Didn't we buy that last week?"

"There's still a little left. Maybe it'll last till next week."

She would have to use money from her private hoard again – precious rands shaved off the precise amounts John gives her to buy bread and milk. Low-fat milk is healthy, she once read in a magazine, so she mixes their milk with a third of boiled water. It doesn't affect the taste and she is helping her family to stay healthy.

She uses this money to buy cosmetics. John had forbidden her to wear make-up; it was the devil's things, he had said when he was still in the throes of ecstasy of his new religion.

"Jessie! Get in here."

Jessie appears wearing a fluffy pink gown. Her sleek black hair falls to her shoulders. She has big brown eyes and full lips. "Yes?"

"Come; help your mother with the shopping list. See what we need. Otherwise, we'll be here until next Sunday."

"What do we need, Mummy?"

"Don't ask her. Look around and see what we need."

Jessie starts opening cupboards to check what's inside.

The hormones in the colony change. This signals the development of alates or primary reproductives. Some grow into kings and others into queens. These grow wings which enable them to fly after the first rains.

Jessie has a boyfriend. Mrs Prinn discovers this by accident. She is emptying the pockets of Jessie's grey trousers before putting them into the washing machine, when she finds a letter. 'Meet me after school' it says in an untidy scrawl. The letter ends with three X's, three kisses. 'Love, Jacob.'

Mrs Prinn contemplates what to do with the letter. Eventually she puts it on the dressing table for her husband to find.

John is furious, as she had anticipated. "What's this?" He waves the letter in front of Jessie's face where she is sitting on the couch painting her toenails a hideous shade of green. Her left foot rests on the coffee table, the toes splayed apart by cotton wool balls wedged between each toe.

"Whoa…?" Jessie pales when she recognises her prized note. "Give it!" She lunges at the note, hopping around on one leg to keep the freshly applied nail polish from smudging. "Give…"

John holds the note aloft, his nostrils flaring. "You will not see this boy anymore, do you hear me?"

"You can't tell me what to do."

"I can and I will. If you continue seeing him, I will ground you for the rest of your life." He stomps out.

"I hate you." Jessie collapses in tears.

Later, Mrs Prinn pretends that she doesn't hear when Jessie sneaks out of the house with a suitcase. John snores loudly. Now and then he stops breathing for a few seconds before continuing with renewed vigour.

Mrs Prinn turns on her other side, covering her head with her pillow. Jessie will be alright, she tells herself. It is the natural order of things. And tomorrow is eviction night on Big Brother Africa; always a good show.

BELINDA

"**B**elinda was sweet. She had a smile for everyone," Oom (uncle) Baba said. He was a tall man with wavy hair smoothed back with ample water and a fingertip of Vaseline. A teacher, he loved to laugh and loved to tell stories.

"She was the youngest of five children, and the queen of her father's heart. At eighteen she had long, slender legs like a filly at the racecourse. With curly black hair, toffee-coloured skin and eyes so dark you could lose yourself in them, she was one of the most beautiful girls around."

Oom Baba paused to sip from a mug of strong black coffee next to his elbow. He assumed the same position when telling his stories: sitting on the bench at the kitchen table with his left arm resting on the table. He used his right hand to paint pictures, to illustrate and add texture to his stories.

Oom Baba continued in his booming voice: "Ey, perhaps it was inevitable that she attracted the attention of one of the stoep sitters. Those scoundrels don't go to school; they won't work, and spend their days following the sun on the stoep outside Nicholson's shop. All they do is play cards, throw dice, and interfere with the people who come to the shop. And Ferdinand was the wildest of the lot.

"He was a pretty man, that Ferdinand. He was dark-dark with an English nose and straight hair that lay down on his forehead like Elvis

Presley. But he was long in the tooth... twenty-eight... and he smoked dagga and drank like a drain. And when he was drunk he thought he was Rambo himself." Oom Baba half raised himself up from the bench. In this crouching position he made stabbing motions with an imaginary knife, his interpretation of Rambo, to drive home his point. He sank down again onto the bench.

"Ja, he had many fights, that Ferdinand. After one of his fights he gained a scar in the shape of a half-moon across his left cheek. After another fight, I forget with whom, the doctors had to operate. They opened his head to remove a piece of his skull and put in a zinc plate. He had a roof in his head." Oom Baba chortled. "Ja, everyone in our dorp talked about the plate in Ferdinand's head. I remember my mother saying to her friends at the church bazaar: 'Just one blow on his head, just one, and he'll be dead.'

"Ferdinand started waylaying Belinda on her daily trips to the shop to buy bread. He would wait for her and insist on carrying the bread while walking her home. But he always stopped about two blocks away from her house. Soon he didn't want to let her go. He entertained her with love songs, holding the bread as ransom."

Oom Baba wagged a finger. "And could he sing! He not only looked like Elvis Presley, he could sing like him too." Oom Baba sang *Are You Lonesome Tonight* and laughed. "That was his song. Then Belinda's father heard about it. You know how it is in a small place. This one talks to that one. That one tells that one. And before you know it, everybody knows everybody's business.

"And our dorpie is small. It's locked in on four sides by a railway station, a koppie, a dam and a tar road. Sort of like a box. The railway station has only two sets of railway lines, coming and going. The koppie – hill – is no more than a whale's hump. The dam was made by someone named Buzan so it's called Buzan's dam, but it's actually a cyanide pit that leaves your skin ashy after a swim. The tar road, a recent addition, brought progress. But, locked in like this, my dorpie breeds close-minded people. Tjo. Everything is bad: dancing, kissing, making love. It's as if everyone living here was born of Immaculate Conception!

"But lemme get back to my story. Belinda's father was a builder. Big and strong, he confronted Ferdinand on Nicholson's stoep. He forbade Ferdinand from speaking to his daughter. 'I'm in love, man,' Ferdinand answered. Belinda's father told him again, swearing this time, that he did not want him to come near his daughter. 'Look at this old toppie,' Ferdinand said to his friends, the riff-raff that spent their days on the stoep instead of working. To Belinda's father, he said, 'What's wrong with you, man? Haven't you ever been in love?'

"Belinda's father answered this by crashing his fist into the dimple on Ferdinand's chin. Ferdinand picked himself up from the floor. 'We're practically family, man,' he said, sounding hurt. 'Family don't fight.' The steam was coming out of Belinda's father's ears by now. 'You useless piece o… shit.'" Oom Baba looked around to see if there were any children listening before he whispered the swear word and laughed. In a louder voice he continued, "'If I catch you near my daughter again, I'll kill you.'

"Next thing we heard, Belinda had run away with Ferdinand and they were getting married. Belinda's father crawled into himself after that. He became quiet. He refused to speak to his daughter and got a stomach ulcer.

"But, you know, the father was also wild in his youth. And he had a cheeky wife, tjo. One day he left in the morning and came home late at night. When he came back there was such a scene. His wife stood in front of him with her hands on her hips, like this." Oom Baba mimicked a teapot with two handles. "Of course she forgave him afterwards. She was not very bright, that one. She left school in standard two.

"But Belinda was good for Ferdinand. He stopped drinking and smoking dagga, and even started working at a printing shop. He lost his hungry look and filled out his clothes more. He looked cleaner than ever before. Ja, he loved Belinda, that Ferdinand. It was there in his eyes when he looked at her.

"He even started his own band. They were popular, and were hired to play at weddings and twenty-first parties. Sometimes they held sessions in the hall. On Saturday nights the young people would pay at the door and dance till dawn. It was the only thing for them to do, except watching football matches on Sundays, of course.

"Against everyone's predictions, they were happy together. They had two children and the children were pretty like the parents. Even Belinda's father came round eventually and gave his blessing. He loved those grandchildren.

"Which just goes to show," Oom Baba drained his mug, spitting out dregs of moerkoffie. He dragged the back of his hand across his mouth. "Love is a funny thing. It's like a toffee; sweet to eat and nice to chew on for the rest of your life.

"But Ferdinand died; yes, he died, after they were married for about four years. Someone hit him with a hammer on his head and – poof – he was dead. They never found out who did it. If you ask me, it's one of those useless chommies of his who still sit on the stoep. And still won't work.

"Belinda, left alone with children to support, became an actress. She was famous. She acted on stage and I saw her once on TV in *Egoli*. Then we heard that she had fallen off a ladder, injuring the right side of her face.

"Then she just disappeared. I don't know what happened to her after that."

KNIT ONE

He had become bigger and Martha had become smaller. It had happened gradually over the years of their marriage, so gradually that she was unaware of it.

One day she awoke and he was inside her body and her mind, filling eighty percent with his presence, edging her out. The weight of him changed her posture. When she was young, she had walked with a light step. Over the years, however, this had changed; her shoulders stooped, her walk slowed.

But she could find relief in their times apart. When he went to work from morning till dusk, she was herself; doing things she liked, when she liked and the way she liked them. Then, she scolded the help incessantly: "Clean the kitchen, Snookie"; "Stop that and do this, Snookie"; "No, Snookie, not like that. How many times must I show you the same thing?"; "Snookie, you're messing up again". Snookie this, Snookie that. The help knew who the supreme commander was.

This ceased, however, when he was home. Then she was ready to please.

"Go make us some tea, Martha."

"With milk or without?" Unpredictable, he varied the way he drank his tea.

On weekends, when Snookie was off and they were alone, he needed her more than ever. "Leave the broom. You can sweep later."

"Of course."

"Come, sit next to me."

"Where, darling?"

"On the couch."

"Can I bring my knitting?"

"I don't like that noise with the knitting needles."

And she would put down the jersey she was making for him. She made one every year, with intricate cable patterns running down the sides. A source of pride; not all could knit a cable jersey. Quietly she followed him to the two-seater couch, a love seat, shuffling one step behind him.

She was but an echo of him. Before giving an opinion, she carefully assessed the situation; where did his views lie? And then she would endorse them. Early in their marriage, she would get it wrong, leading to unpleasantness. But after forty years she was seldom off.

Until death do us part. She liked the permanence of it, the security.

Now he was standing before her, saying something that threatened her being. "I'm going to retire."

"When, dear?"

"At the end of this month. Those bastards can stick their job where the sun don't shine. I've had enough."

"But... but... you're only sixty." She had been counting on another five years of freedom.

"No, I'm tired."

"Oh."

"We have to tighten our belts."

"Of course."

"You have to stop visiting the children so often."

He contributed the money and she had two grown children who had left to start their own lives. She sighed heavily but not audibly; that would be unthinkable.

"Snookie will have to go too," he interrupted her thoughts. "We can do all the housework. We won't need a maid. We'll be here the whole day, doing nothing."

Snookie gone. No. Who would she talk to? She didn't have any friends. He didn't approve of women knit-natting, so she had dismantled her knitting club. At least she would have her two cats. That was a small comfort.

The prospect of having him under her feet the whole day caused a mini-tornado in her heart. When would she clean? Do the washing? The 'we' he was talking about meant her. He considered housework to be a woman's job.

She used to joke with her knitting club that of all her children, he was the most demanding. Now he would be home every single day. A knot of fear spread from her stomach, making her feel weak. She needed to sit down. She couldn't quite bring herself to say, 'yes dear'.

᷎

Five years after his retirement, they were still sitting on the couch. Each had worn a hole – the shape of their bodies – into the fabric. His was bigger, hers smaller; she had shrunk.

Around them the debris of living had piled up: old newspapers, plastic bags from the supermarket, packaging from food, rancid peels. Styrofoam that had contained meat had maggots wriggling in the dried blood. Black algae grew in the fridge. Cat droppings everywhere competed for space. Over it all, a thick layer of dust. Only the couch was clear; a ship, stranded.

Martha sat with a broom in her hand. Her hair had grown long, unkempt. Her narrow shoulders hunched up, swallowing her neck. She made to get up, to lumber to the kitchen.

"No, you can do that later." She sat down again. Between them lay a half-knitted jersey, grimy, the knitting needles coated with rust. "Huh," he said.

"Hah," she said.

"Huh."

"Hah."

COURAGE THE MOUSE

A little brown mouse lived with her family and friends in a rich mielie (corn) field next to a rural village. Like all mice she was always busy, keeping her nose close to the ground as she scurried here and there, looking for things to eat and holes to explore.

One morning, as she came out of her nest in the ground, she heard a strange sound. She stopped to listen, raising her head and twitching her whiskers.

She heard a rumbling, tumbling noise which sounded as if it was coming from far away. So far away, in fact, that she had to concentrate in order to hear it. But once she heard it, it seemed to grow louder until it resounded inside her head. "What is that noise?" she asked one of her brothers.

"What noise? I don't hear anything." Her brother hurried away, continuing his search for food.

The little brown mouse spent the rest of that day asking all the mice she knew whether they could hear the noise. But no one could hear it. The truth was that they didn't stop long enough to listen. It made the little brown mouse uneasy. Was she the only one who could hear the sound?

She decided to ask the Wise Old Tortoise who lived at the bottom of the field. After listening carefully the tortoise put his head to one side and said slowly, "It's the call of destiny." Wise Old Tortoise spoke so slowly that you could finish eating half a mielie between each word.

"Destiny? What's that?"

"It's where to go and what to do with your life."

The little brown mouse thought about what the tortoise had said. "But why am I the only one to hear it?"

"You can't hear it if you always have your nose to the ground. Also, only you can hear it because each one can only ever hear the sound of their own destiny."

The Wise Old Tortoise collapsed after this long speech, his tongue sticking out of the side of his mouth.

"Thank you, wise one," the mouse said.

"Call me Wot for short." Tortoise laughed at his own joke, "Hee-hee-hee." It sounded like he was coughing in slow motion. Embarrassed, the little brown mouse scurried away.

The mouse was curious, so the next day she went to the edge of the mielie field and stood there listening to the sound. She had to know what it was.

She ran a small distance away from the field. Her little heart pounded fearfully as she looked around at the unfamiliar open veld.

Her courage deserted her. She turned back and crashed into something that must have been following her. She squeaked with fright.

"Don't be afraid," she heard someone say. It was Minnie the Meerkat. Minnie was standing upright on her hind legs, looking around. "What are you doing here anyway?"

"I... wanted to... find out where the noise comes from," the mouse stammered, feeling foolish.

"Ah, the sound of the river," Minnie said.

"The river?" the mouse exclaimed in surprise. She was wondering what a river was.

"Yes. Would you like me to take you to the river?" Minnie asked.

"Oh, would you please?" the mouse answered.

She ran next to her new friend. When they went over a rise she saw something shiny not far away. "That's the river," Minnie the Meerkat said. "I stand up now and then to look around so I know where things are."

"Thanks." The mouse was so excited that she ran on alone.

The rumbling became louder. The river! She gasped in awe. It was beautiful. The water was tumbling over rocks, causing white foam bubbles which fell and broke in a stream of blue-green water.

Bullfrog was sitting on a round leaf in the water. "Hello there," he called in a deep voice. When he spoke, air moved the bottom part of his lip in and out, in and out. "What is your name?"

"I don't have a name," the mouse answered.

"Will you do something for me?" Bullfrog asked. "Crouch down as low as you can then jump as high as you can."

The mouse thought that this was a silly request but she did not want to offend a new friend. So she crouched as low as she could and jumped as high as she could; and fell plop into the water. "Oh, you are wicked," cried the little mouse, desperately clutching at the long grass growing on the side of the river.

Bullfrog laughed and laughed. "But what did you see?" he asked.

The mouse climbed out and sat thinking for a moment. "I think I saw something in the distance," she said.

"That's Thaba-Nchu, the black mountain. Do you want to see the mountain?"

"No," said the mouse. She had had enough. She turned and ran home as fast as she could.

"You have a name now," Bullfrog called after her. "It's Courage."

At home Courage tried to tell the other mice about the river, but they would not believe her. They were also afraid because she was wet and it had not been raining. So they started avoiding her. Courage was sad.

She sat alone, listening to the river and thinking about the black mountain. Then she decided to look for the mountain. She left the mielie field and scurried across the open veld.

"Psst," she heard someone call. She saw a tawny lion hiding behind a bush.

"Who are you and why are you hiding?" she asked.

"I'm Mr Lion and I'm afraid of the mother over there." Courage noticed an elephant nearby. It was as big as a house. "I scared her baby," Mr Lion whispered. "Don't you want to scare her off so she will go away please?"

"You're joking, right?"

"No. Do you know that elephants are afraid of mice?"

"Haikona, no."

"Well, they are. All you have to do is run in front of them. Ready, steady, go!"

Courage darted in front of the elephant. It screamed in a high-pitched voice and ran away, ears flapping, the ground shaking. Scared out of her socks, Courage sprinted to a nearby rock.

"Do you know what that shadow is?" she heard a voice saying. She looked up and saw that the 'rock' was an old black buffalo. In front of them hovered a shadow with outstretched wings.

"No, sir."

"It's a hawk," the buffalo continued. "If it sees you, you are dead. By the way my name is Ben."

"Pleased to meet you. What should I do about the hawk?" Courage asked, worried.

"I will help you if you help me," Ben Buffalo said. "I'm lying here because I'm blind and cannot see. If you give me your eyes, you can walk under my body and be safe."

Courage thought about it. She did not want to give away her eyes, but she was more afraid of the hawk. Eventually she said, "Alright."

As soon as she said it, her eyes closed and she could not see. Ben walked across the veld with Courage running underneath him.

Without her eyes Courage found that she relied more and more on her other senses: hearing, smell, touch and taste. They travelled for many days. Her senses were especially acute by the time they reached the mountain.

Here Ben Buffalo said: "I must leave now. You have to go up alone." Courage sat quivering with fear. She was alone and she could not even see where she was! "Just follow your instinct." Ben walked away.

Slowly, carefully, Courage climbed the mountain. She stopped often to think about where she was going and what to do next. When she reached the top she was ecstatic.

Then she heard the sound of flapping wings. The hawk! The flapping came nearer and nearer until she imagined she could feel the black shadow hovering above her back.

Swoop! Something struck her and she felt herself soaring. The hawk was carrying her away! She uttered a shrill squeak which was very loud because of her great fear.

The sound of her cry seemed to bounce back, to come back at her. She dived instinctively. That was when she realised she was flying. "I can fly! I can fly," she said.

"Yes, you can," a voice said. "I'm Ra, the Sun-god of Egypt, the place where all the African tribes come from. We're on our way to the sun. When we get there, you're going to help me sail my boat across the sky, while I carry the sun on my head."

STOLEN

I went for a walk in my pyjamas with my hair unbrushed. Ensnared in my thoughts I slipped away from the present; walking without thinking, without seeing.

I probably took a wrong turn, I don't remember, but now I was in a strange place, tired, my anxiety increasing with each step.

Lamp poles had posters for penis enlargement glued around their midriffs like miniskirts. These poles dislodged themselves from the ground and stomped the dance of Africa, carrying their lights as colourful headdresses representing all the nations of the continent.

Ahead, a dilapidated building with a huge sign that read 'Universal Church of God'. The building dipped and bowed, holding out its roof upside down, a giant collection plate. A proliferation of private churches dotted the landscape. Every person could open his own church.

A beggar appeared. He made the sign of the cross and started praying. With his lips still moving in audible prayer, he moved between the rows of cars. His blue eyes challenged me. I was intruding on his domain.

My heart beat faster; my throat was like a desert. I must look confident, as if I know where I'm going. This advice, given to me long ago by my deceased father, resonated in my head. I repeated it like a mantra, trying to push down the rising panic as I hurried on.

The second toe on my left foot went into spasm, forcing me to stand awhile. People were coming into the street on their way to work. My early morning walk had lasted longer than I had anticipated. I tried to smooth down my hair. It had a life of its own; I needed a brush to tame it.

I searched again. Nothing was familiar. In fact, I had strayed into a poor neighbourhood. Here the people didn't look busy and preoccupied. Here they stopped to stare at me; unfriendly stares that didn't invite enquiry.

Asking for directions would advertise that I was lost, maybe instigating an attack. Their hostility was palpable. I plunged on, walking into the direction I was facing. Turning back would be suicide.

I'm at the graveyard at my own funeral hiding among the tombstones; tired of running, my chest is burning.

I came into a cul-de-sac. In front of me the blackened walls of a burnt-out house. I darted into it to get away from the stares. Blind fear gripped me as I realised that I was trapped. I let out a sound like a sob. Somebody came up behind me and then I was no more.

I came to in a house surrounded by women dressed in long scarves and saris. Crying with relief, I sat up. Where was I? One of the women said I was in a place that was unfamiliar.

"I got lost," I sobbed.

"Are you from…?" She enquired, mentioning the place I was visiting with my husband and children.

"Yes," I garbled eagerly. I was saved. Obviously they knew the area where I was from and would shortly deliver me there. "My children must be wondering where I am." This was said with the knowledge of being among women. Silence followed. "Can I go now? Back to…?"

"You have to wait for my husband."

I'm at the graveyard at my own funeral hiding among the tombstones; someone is chasing me.

Her husband appeared. He informed me that he had found me with one of his workers and had moved me into his house. I had been asleep for three days. I looked down at my body. I was wearing a black sleeveless top and blue jeans. Who had undressed me? Strangers had been looking at my body without my knowledge.

"May I go now, please?"

"You'd better talk to my wife."

My stomach churned. "Call her for me, please?"

"Certainly." He left and his wife returned.

I'm at the graveyard at my own funeral hiding among the tombstones and I'm deathly afraid.

Her demeanour had changed. She was no longer friendly. "I should tell you straightaway. You're not free to go."

"But, why?" Tears choked my voice.

"Because we bought you, we paid money for you. You are here now. You have to stay."

"My children…"

"Forget about your children. Here, take another tablet." She handed me a clear, gel-like capsule in the shape of a roof. I felt rising hysteria. "Drink it. It will make you feel better."

Taking the cup with water she proffered, I faked putting the pill into my mouth and took a big gulp of water. "There." She left, closing the door.

For the first time I looked around. There was a kennel in the corner on a raised mound of earth; my place to sleep. The same red earth covered the floor, only compacted down more firmly.

DD GOES TO HOSPITAL

He sat on a bench, tall, gaunt, his head forward, cradling his injured hand. He had come for a dressing; orders from the doctor who saw him after he had burned himself over an open fire a week ago.

The nurse attending to him saw that the white lice from his body had colonised the bandage. She let out a squeal, disappeared behind a curtain. Young, petite, with spindly legs, she peeped out, disappeared again.

He sat there waiting. Living on the street had made him patient. Eventually someone would come and attend to him; it was his right.

Helen Joseph Hospital had green walls and floors. It had belonged to the whites first, but now it catered to all races. In this process it had changed from its bright cleanliness, which could still be seen here and there, into its current grubby look. A trolley screeched somewhere, needing oil.

His hand throbbed, a dull ache. Ask for Panados, he reminded himself. Memory had receded with his hairline. He stared at the curtain. Where were these people? He had been waiting now for more than half an hour.

Footsteps approached. His other hand moved over the bandage protectively. Black with soot, it had patches of yellow where pus had seeped through. Opening and closing his fist, he tried to encourage the lice to move back up his tattered sleeve into the seams of his clothing where they had come from. However, they seemed to burrow deeper into the bandage.

A fat woman dressed in pink stripes appeared. Her legs, like tree stumps, were encased in shiny stockings.

"No-o," he mumbled. "Ugly as the day is long."

"Who're you talking to?"

"Nobody."

"Cheeky, are we? You come here with your lice and nobody wants to change your bandage. The nurse ran away. She refuses to come back. And because I'm the assistant nurse, the one with no qualifications, I've been told to come. What nonsense is that? But let me get one thing straight. I'm not taking any of your—" She grabbed his hand.

"Eina!" He jerked it back, held it in front of his big grey head.

"Listen here. I don't have time for this. Duh-you want me to change your dressing? Yes or no."

Gingerly he held out his hand towards her, a grimace distorting his withered face, showing yellow rotting teeth.

"You stink." Standing as far from him as she could, she unwound the bandage. The part on the wound was stuck.

"If you wet it, it will come off," he said.

"I don't need your advice. Who duh-you think you are?"

She ripped it off in one swift movement, causing the new tissue underneath to bleed. She threw the bandage into a brown paper bag she had stuck onto a trolley with tape. Lice fell on the floor. The shock of the cold floor caused them to run in all directions, looking for shelter, for warmth. She screamed, stamping them with her foot, and then started scratching wildly. "I'm itching. After this I'll need a bath. And for all I know, you have Aids too." She looked at his blood in distaste.

Burning his hand, that was a stupid thing to do, he thought, as he watched her clean the wound with a spray bottle. But it had been a freezing night and he had been cold, so cold that he needed to touch the fire of cardboard boxes to get warm. Now he would have to be subjected to this treatment until the wound healed.

The contents of the bottle had a strong chemical smell. He tried to read the label. If he collected enough money at the parking lot where he worked as a car guard, waving people in and out of a parking bay, he could maybe buy it from the chemist and change the dressing himself.

She put the spray bottle down and applied shiny brown ointment with a spatula. Afterwards, she wound the bandage around his thumb and the palm of his hand, securing it with tape.

"I'm not what you think. I have a master's in education. I was an inspector."

She snorted. "If you're so educated, how come you live on the street?"

He winced. "It's a long story."

"Keep it to yourself. I don't want to hear it. You people all have some story or other. And I'm not listening to sob stories. I'm not a social worker."

"I'll need some Panado, for pain," he said.

"Where's your bed letter?"

He gave her the hospital file.

"What's your name?"

"DD." He had inherited his great-grandfather's name and surname, but had always just been known as DD. Born on 7 July, 1950, he shared his birthday with the arrival of the Group Areas Act and the Population Registration Act.

"That's a girl's name?"

"No." He didn't feel like explaining that he didn't feel worthy of his great-grandfather's name and had shortened it to only the initials. One day he would be worthy. But hope was running out; he was almost sixty-three. Meanwhile, he needed painkillers.

She opened the file. "The doctor didn't write up any Panado for you."

"No. Please. I need…" he trailed off as she walked away.

You witch, thought the old man. Panados are cheap. You can buy them over the counter at any chemist. He could see her retrieving a mop and a bucket from a cupboard. He could hear her, too, laughing.

"Smelly old pig," she said. "I've got to disinfect where he sat and where he touched."

He'll show her. When he saw her returning, he fell to his knees, crawling on the floor to look for the fallen lice. Each one he found he tucked into his shirt. He heard a gasp behind him.

"Hey! What you doing? You can't do that!"

"They're my lice," he said. "They want to come home with me!"

"Get out of here." She pushed the bucket against his leg with such force that the antiseptic spilled onto his soiled jeans.

"You stupid idiot." He got up, stumbled away limping. "How dare you treat me like this? I'm a human being. The new South Africa means nothing because it's populated by people like you. People with no respect. Mandela sacrificed himself for nothing. And you probably didn't even pass standard eight, you fat slob."

"Hey voetsek, get lost, with your master's," she said. "If you're kamma – really, so educated, how come you live on the street? Jou slegte ding. (You bad thing.) Security!"

She waggled to the entrance, shouting again. "Security!"

Those waiting on the benches sniggered.

COFFEE

As she came out of the pharmacy she noticed the coffee shop. Red and yellow tables and chairs, benches, were outside a high counter. She hadn't had breakfast.

I don't like this place.

She neared the counter, the assistant moved closer. Under his scrutiny she tried to read the small print describing their fare. Nearsighted, she frowned in concentration, intensely aware of the hovering figure just outside her peripheral vision.

Making up her mind about food was a slow process. She studied the scone, tasted it on her tongue. It was too big and looked floury. The chicken mayonnaise sandwich was a possibility, but sometimes the chicken was rubbery. She couldn't see butter in the ham and cheese croissant. Her eyes moved back to the scone. The assistant waited.

After a while she felt moved to say, "I'm still looking." She was now bound to order. She studied the food again with renewed interest. Still unsure, but under the silent pressure of the assistant, she ordered the ham and cheese sandwich.

He put it on a plate and asked her to wait at one of the tables for her coffee.

Selecting a table where she could watch the people walking past, she bit into the sandwich. No butter. Picking at the dryness with her fingers, she waited for her coffee.

He motioned to her to come to the counter to collect it.

Immediate anger flooded her system. If she was white he would've brought it to her table. Her anger must've shown on her face because when she approached him, he said, "Hau." He asked if she wanted milk, handed her the cup. She realised that he was a foreigner.

The coffee was good, made up for the dry sandwich. She turned her attention to the people. That one there looked like a drug addict; painfully thin, disfiguring marks on her face caused by tik. She was just sitting on a bench, looking into a clothing shop.

Two or three people arrived, ordered from the counter, went to get their coffee. They got their own coffee! And these were white people. Immediate remorse and shame. She cursed the sensitisation of apartheid that had been bred into her. Growing up, she had developed a finely tuned sixth sense to detect racism as soon as possible in order to mount a defence; fight or flight.

Do others also carry this protection like a tortoise shell, ready to disappear into it at the first provocation even if they are mistaken? Was she not an apartheid addict then, hooked on self-preservation?

The assistant would think she was displaying xenophobia; that ugly word that had provided numbing pictures of violence in the newspapers recently. She ventured to look at him. He was casting upset glances in her direction.

She cursed her subconscious mind. It didn't know that it was in the new South Africa. It just reacted and landed her in trouble without as much as a consultation; reducing her to the level of an organism responding to a stimulus.

Huh? I don't feel safe.

She liked to think that consciously she would never have made the decision to be angry.

A new assistant arrived. The incumbent came out from behind the counter; he was on a break. As he walked past, he looked at her with venom.

AN EPITAPH

From time to time I indulge in a stately dance with Lady Luck. We gently embrace and I smile as we glide to the slot machines, turn at the roulette, or twirl at the blackjack.

No frantic quickstep swinging to and fro, breathing fast, sweat pouring down my brow into my eyes, burning and obscuring my sight. That's not for me. Oh no. That's the compulsive gambler. And there is no fun in doing anything compulsively; working yourself up into a frenzied tango and ending up on a psychiatrist's couch.

No siree. I enjoy waltzing with Lady Luck and she has always been kind to me. Have you noticed how you win when you are in a good mood? But the minute you become agitated and twist your psyche into a knot, Lady Luck deserts you, taking your money with her.

And believe me there is nothing to rival her kiss. That rush of adrenaline, that surge of euphoria, soothes the wrinkles of care, and injects a memorable moment into even the dullest life.

That is why I lie here.

At 35, slain by a kiss.

THE MAN

The man went into the house, a woman came out. The man was no longer in the house.

WHAT'S WRONG?

1. You're so quiet, geez lighten up. We're going for a nice drive.
2. No, we're not running away from the police. Whatever gave you that idea?
3. People like to talk. Don't believe anything you hear about me.
4. You know me, I love children. The whole world knows I love children.

BEGOOGLED

Depressed, she sat in front of her computer. She typed 'broken heart' into the search box, and then read what came up. *Images of broken heart.* She liked the fifth one; a cartoon heart with a jagged line across the centre with the word 'why' in the middle. Indeed, why did he break her heart? All she ever wanted was to love him. *Quotes about broken hearts.* She didn't want to read the thoughts of some writer whose heart had never been broken quite like hers. *Wikipedia.* Who needed the definition of a broken heart? She knew that too well already. *How to fix a broken heart; Broken heart SMS collection; 3 ways to heal a broken heart.*

This looked promising. *Broken heart syndrome; you can die of a broken heart. 'In broken heart syndrome, a part of your heart temporarily enlarges and doesn't pump well, while the rest of your heart functions normally or with even more forceful contractions. Researchers are just starting to learn the causes, and how to diagnose and treat it.'* (American Heart Association)

She knew it. That fool was playing with her life. She read the symptoms: chest pain, shortness of breath, irregular heartbeats. She knew he would kill her one day. *'Tests show ballooning and unusual movement of the lower left heart chamber (left ventricle).'* It would serve him right if she died. He would be crippled by guilt.

She felt a searing chest pain, couldn't breathe, felt how her right ventricle was enlarging, or was it the left one? Clutching her chest, she reached for the phone, dialled 911.

In the overcrowded, under-resourced and understaffed hospital, the doctor on call refused to listen to her pleas. Her request for the blood and other cardiac tests mentioned online were ignored.

A few days later she died. Consider this: she had a pre-existing heart defect, or she had latent heart disease. The attack was brought on by autosuggestion and extreme stress, or, it would've happened anyway.

THE INVISIBLE PERSON

A man heard a sound. He got up, fetched his gun. He shot the intruder through the window. Years of gun ownership and training paying off, he killed him.

But there was an accident; his daughter had sneaked out to use his car, wandering into a forbidden space, where only violence can follow. Whisper: Not only usurping the thief's place, but also his destiny. The law upheld the defence of trying to shoot an invader. He was not prosecuted, his grief deemed enough punishment.

New mothers teach their daughters that they are free and can achieve whatever they want.

Sometimes you see him, sometimes you don't. Peek-a-boo; he's playing a game. He lurks in the room, eating breakfast with you, going to work or school with you, wearing a long-sleeved shirt, formal trousers and a tie. Carrying his lunch box, he job shadows you, learning your trade, trying to oust you, without you ever speaking to him except in your thoughts. He exists by watching you. He is the invisible person.

He attends dinner parties; rudely he monopolises conversation. Every Tom Dick and Jenkins talks about him, to him, saying thank God at least he didn't slaughter you. Omnipresent, he follows just one step behind, close enough to invade your personal space; that space that should be sacrosanct. He plagues your dreams, your nightmares and your waking moments. High walls, metal spikes, razor and electric wire do not deter him. In the room with you, he waits to rob you, assault and kill you.

Most fathers teach their sons that women are to be controlled.

He shot his girlfriend. Where exploration of new love should have been, tragedy lurked. Generations of gun training enabled him to track her as she fell.

An accident; he feared for his life. And fear accompanies the sound of the phantom. Whisper: Whenever he is heard, never seen, fear is next to him casting a white pall over his dark shadow. You have to obliterate him to be safe. A valid defence.

Women raped in training camps.

Where are the ones who followed orders during apartheid, killing and maiming on command? They are hiding in families who don't know what they are capable of, until they braai someone on coals or a discarded tyre; accepted warfare. Whisper: Can you take the war out of a soldier?

Babies and young girls raped at home.

A visitor from another land allegedly killed his new wife. He was disinclined to marry and she was in his way. He travelled to lap at our shores of fear.

One thousand women killed every year by an intimate partner.

A sound came from the bathroom. The door opened, startling the homeowner who had gone to investigate. He fired. His wife fell to the floor.

Where did he come from, this ghost, this phantom? Some say that he is a seasoned traveller, having glided through three and a half centuries.

Separate development, everyone advancing at their own pace; a policy that had to be brutally enforced, hidden from the glance of the electorate who preferred to close their eyes and believe in the threat, the dark ghost. The past is creeping into the future on stealthy legs, refusing to be broken. Twenty years on, and everyone is in their laager of townhouses to escape the phantom.

Why is a man's life more valuable than a woman's?

She wanted to leave him and he hired four to rape her, had her nipple twisted off with pliers. He killed her son; shot him like a springbok for its tender meat. Her crime was referring to his inadequacy in bed; a capital offence. Torture and violence reserved for those without power.

Why does a man call a weaker man a woman as an insult?

Violent land of my heart, heavy is the burden of the conqueror. Fear resembling anger, silently growing, deadly, and ready to explode. Something that cannot be talked about, it is submerged, whispered when people gather.

The rain of patriarchy has saturated the land; each tribe or race, having forgotten their umbrellas, caught in the deluge.

QUEST FOR MY DIGNITY

I've been on a lifelong search for my dignity, but it eludes me. Every time we are in the same place, I reach out, but it jumps up like some small startled animal and runs away.

The first time it happened I was on a train with my father. We had just disembarked and were waiting for another train. Where we lived, on the outskirts of Johannesburg, we had to get two trains to reach town; one to Langlaagte and then a different one to town.

While waiting at the Langlaagte station, a white policeman came up and talked to my father in an aggressive manner. In my thirteen-year-old mind, I couldn't see what our transgression had been. The policeman was young, in blue uniform with a club on his belt.

My first response was surprise. What did we do to warrant such a thing? I was quizzically looking at him, trying to guess at what was happening when my father started apologising. "Asseblief my baas. Please, boss. We're just waiting for the train."

Instead of placating the policeman, this spurred him on and he unleashed a new torrent of abuse. He was speaking to my father. The man I looked up to and adored. Although only thirteen, I knew that he was humiliating my father and rejoicing in it.

A searing anger filled my heart. Hitherto, an avid reader with no access to stories about my own people, I had been reading books for white people and cultivated an outlook with an awareness of my rights.

Surely this was wrong. How dare a young man speak to an older man like that? My indignance rose. Didn't he have any manners? I shook with fury. "That is enough," I said to the young man. He stopped and looked at me in disbelief. Before he could respond, my father started grovelling: "Asseblief my baas. Groot baas," and dragged me away.

I was ashamed of my father. I looked at him and suddenly he had grown smaller. I didn't know that his first instinct was to protect me. And that he would do whatever was required, even humiliate himself. I had never met that side of his love before. Hitherto, I had only seen the smiling, nurturing side.

On the way home we didn't speak much. I could see that he was embarrassed. In witnessing my father losing his dignity, my own was diminished.

We never spoke about it afterwards. He didn't reprimand me or explain. It just slipped into the trough of things not talked about.

In my innocence, I was proud of myself. Someone had insulted my father and I had stood up for him. Mixed in with my displaced pride was the first crinkle of my existence as a black person in South Africa. The values I had imbibed from books didn't apply to me. *The Famous Five, Trompie and Saartjie* were from another planet. There were different laws that governed my existence. And in them was no thought about my dignity.

Rape
He took my pride
abused me
pushed protests aside
misused me
extinguished the light

inside me
tainted my own sight
of what's me.

He took my life
before me
no longer a wife
(he's ashamed of me)
an anchorite
he made me
in just one night
destroyed me.

It was my first child. A needle set in the crook of my arm, plaster, fluid running cold into my vein; my resolve not to scream forgotten.

Okay, I won't scream but I will moan. It sounded like somebody else. In a line-up of shrieks I wouldn't recognise mine. A stranger had taken over my body; a stranger who wasn't shy to groan. Shut up, I said.

Answered questions, when it started, how long it lasts. I put on a short white gown, open at the back, not bothering to close the blue-green curtain. Pain, a dull ache, started in the small of my back. It moved down, burning, gathering strength, in my sacrum. It radiated to my stomach. I pressed my fingers deep into my groin to massage the pain. First, a gentle squeeze at my womb's lower end, and then an iron grip reached up to my sternum.

A man at the next bed; he didn't belong there. He was drunk, snoring upright on a bench.

I noticed a cockroach as I shoved my bag – packed according to the hospital pamphlet – into the locker. Kneeling on the floor until the pain abated, I didn't care who saw me. In my world of pain there was no space for shame. Vast, it stretched from ceiling to floor, from wall to wall.

Another cycle: back, sacrum, lower abdomen, sternum. Like music, a regular rhythm. No rest in-between.

My arm tingled, the oxytocin drip too fast. What are you trying to do, kill me? Where's the doctor? What did you say? Not here, still coming. Moaning doesn't help. Three minutes feel like seconds, not enough time to stitch my fortitude. The light's too bright. Okay, breathe.

A gloved hand swivelled inside me, fingers clawing a long time. An examination; a stretch and sweep.

Breathing wasn't helping. Whose idea was it to breathe at a time like this anyway? The desire to push so strong, stronger than the brain saying breathe. What? Breathe? I am breathing! And I'm going to die if I don't obey my body. Back, sacrum, lower abdomen, sternum; the pain stretched my pelvic floor, my stomach harder than a cricket ball.

Why are you shouting? And why are you swearing? I'd changed from a gentle person into a harridan, just like the pain. It had started gently and now it was breaking my body apart. He was still there, the stranger; why didn't he go home? Or was it a mirage? My moans built to a crescendo; the womb a muscle that would grow thin and tear rather than stop. Primitive nature took over, heeding no one.

Swollen, like a wheel. The swelling would go down in two to three days. In the meantime it was difficult to walk. I had to hang onto the walls for support.

"You have an opportunistic infection," the doctor said. "Your CD4 count is low."

It was like a blow to my chest.

"There's fluid in your lungs. We'll have to drain it. Tell me, why did you stop coming for your treatment?"

I had no answer, recalling my healing by the great Benny Hinn. He had come to South Africa on a cold, rainy day. I had queued for hours under an umbrella which kept off the rain but not the faint mist that sifted down around it, leaving me cold and wet.

Eventually we were seated. I sat in the section of the ill, close to the stage where we could go up for an anointing. Around me desperate people, some in wheelchairs, others carried in by friends and relatives.

When the service started I was giddy with relief. I prepared myself. I sang. I prayed, swaying with intensity and weakness. I sat down. I stood up. Still we prayed. I listened to five sermons – wedged inbetween the band playing and the singing – about giving. God gave to those who gave to His church.

Someone passed cards around for our bank details and an amount to pledge each month. I filled it in. I cried. I waited.

At last it was time to go onto the stage. We filed in queues, helped by ushers. I was so far from the stage I was worried that I would not get there with so many people around.

We crowded forward, our eyes wet with tears of expectation. Just when I reached the steps that led to the stage, someone stepped in front of me, his arms outstretched. I looked up. Benny Hinn had disappeared.

An announcement was made. He had healed enough for one day. The rest of us would have to come back another time. A man on a stretcher started sobbing. I tried to reason with the huge man blocking my way. I have to see him, I said. I've come from far. I will not be able to come again.

Again I was thirteen years old, pleading to be seen, to be recognised as a person with dignity. Again my dignity and I were not in the same place. It'd deserted me when I needed it most. My pleas fell on indifferent ears. I followed the throng of the returning ill, exhausted.

Benny Hinn never laid hands on me but still I believed that I had been healed. I didn't need medication as long as I believed, if my faith was strong enough. I thanked the Lord every day for my healing. I went to church. I donated my tenth to the Lord's church, but the coughing and diarrhoea did not stop.

Soon I became short of breath.

AKERE

3.

In the land of the shape-shifters there were only women. They had a peculiar way of sitting, leaning back in a chair, their arms outstretched and opened wide in a welcoming gesture. Their legs, too, were stretched out, open; curved gently at the knees to form a silent O. In this posture they would sit for hours, even during a conversation.

Everyone's legs were extremely thin, as legs tend to be if they bear no weight.

Their country had the figure of a lopsided heart with a strip cut out. On the east of Akere, for that was its name, was a region which was spherical, and on the west an area which was unknown. These countries nudged the Antagon Sea, a roiling mass of water and black rocks.

Akere had red trees, white elephants, green monkeys and purple birds. On the forest floor grew a variety of insect-eating plants. The elephants were white because they covered themselves with soil as protection against gnats. The monkeys didn't reach adulthood; they remained soft and cuddly as teddy bears.

The creatures of the sphere Mamela, half deer, half man, had annexed the missing piece of the Akerian domain, a long sash which ran diagonally across its western border. They'd appeared one morning during the rains, migrating in droves, carrying huge antlers and lethal kicks. A tent city had sprung up. Meeting no opposition, they had fenced off the area.

The Akerish people had been taken by surprise. Expecting no enemy from the inhospitable sea or The Unknown (which was said to be unpopulated), and having a friendly neighbour, or so they thought, they had no army.

Hurt by the aggressive act which was against their expectations, they'd pleaded but were ignored. The invasion had resulted in severe sulking, not least because the deer-men spent hours urinating on their antlers to mark their occupied territory.

Artemis had been in her late teens when they arrived. She was busy baking, her hands floury. She'd run outside in her apron. "Hoi, did you see that?" she'd said to those standing next to her. Many hooves had raised the dust to a fine film. The smell of musk had been overwhelming. It had tickled her nose to a sneeze.

The deer-men had paraded two abreast, lifting up their front hooves in a stiff-legged strut. About three hundred of them, they'd marched to the beat of a monkey drum, made by stretching the prepared skin of a monkey tight over stuffed elephant trunks. "They have our drums. Where did they get one of our drums? They stole it! We have to stop them. They're taking our land." Artemis had brandished her cake roller.

Everyone had stood where they were. "C'mon, please, we have to do something." However, trying to rally the Akerians to resist had been futile. A passive people, they'd watched, admiring the spectacle of magnificent antlers.

"You hound! Go back to your own land." Artemis had charged into the nearest one, a huge stag. She'd hit him on the rump. He'd lifted her with his antlers and tossed her back into the crowd. Bruised, crying, Artemis had witnessed them marching further and further into her country.

She had cried at the invasion of her beautiful land, where the female purple birds guarded the nests while their mates sat on it to hatch the eggs. Gregarious, these birds paired off with four males at a time and had quite a job looking after their nests.

Now, five years older, Artemis had a permanent frown. Streaks of grey hair had appeared the morning after the deer-men had arrived. Overcome by anxiety, she had a recurring dream. In her dream she was lost and asked everybody she met how to get home but they all betrayed her. A medical student was on the way to the dance hall; another resident had just had a manicure and was trying to decide between red lipstick and clear lip gloss. One offered her a lift, but tried to grab her handbag. A feeling of alienation, of not being able to reach anyone, coloured the dream. A rising desperation. They wouldn't stop; they were too busy.

In her nightmare she was in a strange city, next to the sea and a mountain jutting out like a breast. Although at first the place appeared familiar, this was dispelled at closer inspection, and she wandered aimlessly, trying to be friendly and ingratiating to induce kindness. A young woman led her down a hole where all the buildings were covered with dirty brown water up to their eaves. When Artemis said she couldn't swim, the young woman and her friends made rude remarks about her age.

Usually, the shape-shifters flitted past at lightning speed, not solidifying into a concrete being unless summoned. They were the ghosts of the land; sometimes blue, sometimes black, and all the shades in-between. But Artemis knew they were the most intuitive; perfect for interpreting her dream.

She bought a ghost-snare at the market; a silver halo with grey netting. Walking into the woods, she avoided the flesh-eating plants which grew in stunted bushes, and almost stumbled into an elephant cow nursing her calf. The mother trumpeted loudly, waving her ears. Artemis apologised. After a terrifying display, the elephant calmed down and accepted her apology with gentle snorts from its trunk.

Artemis' C-shaped back, the result of sitting in a particular posture for decades, trembled. She was so close to the elephant she could see the chalky dust on its sides. These giants had a reputation for crushing people. Slowly the elephant moved away.

She cast her net about. Her legs were covered in white dust up to her knees. A group of monkeys peered from a tree, chattering. They came down to touch her cape, pulling at it, playing. They were green and had yellow eyes. Artemis shook them off. Squealing loudly, they returned to their perch in the tree.

She watched out for the one-eyed iguanas. These small round animals hid in the long grass. An iguana bounced up, closed its tiny teeth around the index finger of her right hand. She swung it about, trying to dislodge the iguana, but it held on. "Off! Off!" She pulled at its body. Its tail came off in her hand. She flung it on the grass. The tail wriggled like a worm. She stamped on it with her red boots. Blood mixed with white flesh stained the grass. An insect plant nearby leaned over and scooped up the morsel. Although its main diet was insects, it relished the occasional treat.

She slapped at the green gnats that buzzed around her face, threatening to go into her mouth. Competing with the raucous mating calls of the purple birds, she chanted: "Shape-shifter, shape-shifter. Please come to me."

It was a dangerous activity. Sometimes an irate shape-shifter would land up in the net and boil out with frenzied slaps and kicks at being disturbed. There were stories of a shape-shifter breaking someone's teeth. Once, a shape-shifter even killed someone by poking a finger in an eye.

Rumours flourished that they cast spells. A vicious spell caused you to lose your appetite. Another made you lose your hair. Artemis was fond of her waves, which had never seen a comb. She also loved the Akerian diet of red tree leaves, elephant's milk, roasted gnats and purple chicken, which had, before her visions, given her a much-desired peach shape.

"Shape-shifter, shape-shifter. Please come to me." Artemis almost dropped the net when she heard a sscroosh. Something heavy had landed in the net. She peered at it. Before her eyes it flowed out of the net to stand in front of her. The shape-shifter was dark blue, almost black, to indicate its status as having lost its body. It flowed into different shapes; a tree, a bush, a big gnat.

Nearly sobbing with fear she relayed her dream. Of undetermined gender, a seer, it interpreted her prescience. "The stick-legged women are too vulnerable on account of their posture. And their propensity to speak in a language that rational beings do not understand. A plan must be made to rehabilitate them." It spoke in whispers like the wind.

Before she could answer, the shape-shifter melted away. Artemis slapped her net about angrily, cursing. Sleepless nights had reduced her to a sylph, and it gave her that gobbledegook? There was nothing wrong with their posture. All of them had been sitting like that for generations. Ever since the first Akerian, Zika, had crossed the unknown on a flying monkey to populate the land. And to suggest that something was wrong with their mother tongue was spurious. Akerish was a language of gentle tones and sibilant sighs. Who wouldn't understand such a language?

All this thrashing about, using a word which was but one letter less than 'shift' and close in sound, awakened another shape-shifter. Hard of hearing, it appeared in her net, ready to help.

"Far out," it said. "Do ya have any weed?" It flowed repeatedly into the same shape, a dagga bush. Artemis was not in the mood for trivialities. She screamed at it, telling it to get lost.

"Ith thith groovy or what?" the shape-shifter lisped, scratching its royal-blue head. Clearly, it didn't understand her attitude. "Exthuse me, thomeone called, right?" Ripples of agitation shook the dagga bush. Artemis knew she had been rude but she was too upset to apologise. The shape-shifter's big lemur eyes, black pools of confusion, were fixed on her face. "Thomeone called me, yeth?" And now it was faced with a woman whose body matched her legs, unusual in the species, telling it to scram. It did what any self-respecting shape-shifter would do under such circumstances. It tickled her ears.

Artemis giggled uncontrollably. She begged it to stop. "Far out, man," it said as it disappeared. Her ego bruised at her lack of decorum, she hurried away, vowing never again to listen to what people say. Lying was inherent to the human condition. All the stories about the shape-shifters assaulting people were bogus. She had antagonised a shape-shifter until it trembled, and it had not hurt her.

On her long walk home, she reflected on the encounter. The first shape-shifter had confused her. The second one, well, it was a lunatic, but the first… All she'd wanted was to understand why she always appeared lost in her dream and instead it had offered her a puzzle. She was an artist, for crying out loud, riddles gave her a headache.

Most of the citizens in Akere had copies of her red trees on white soil, with lopsided hearts hovering around the edges. She earned a good living. Deciding to ignore the shape-shifter's ramblings, she threw herself into a new painting of an elephant performing a mock charge.

But the dream wouldn't go away. Night after night it plagued her, leaving her ill and exhausted. She was reluctant to inconvenience herself with the burden of rehabilitating anybody. Already the people of Akere crossed the road when they saw her. What if she still tried to talk to them? No. She preferred to read and to think. Her relationship with Ma and her sister, Micky, was strained. She regarded women as fractious, fickle and fallow.

The dream was draining her strength. Soon she would expire if she didn't heed the call. For that was what it was; a plea for her to step up and rescue her people. She had realised that during a particularly restless night. She hadn't slept at all. The dawn saw her red-eyed and grim. A thought flitted in and out. She caught it just as it was leaving, straining to bring it back. That quiet thought, which she had almost missed, told her what she needed to know.

The shape-shifters were the exiled ghosts of the women in her country. They were waiting, eternally waiting, to be reunited with their owners' bodies. When the owner died, they became blue-black. These shape-shifters were on a higher plane than the ones who still had bodies, the blue and grey ones. Some of them held back the ocean from swamping the land, while others became seers. Could she ignore the advice of such a medium?

Pimply with reluctance, she summoned her resolve. She would have to cast about for a strategy. What would it take to rehabilitate women? It was a question beyond her imagination. She decided to ask The Ruler, a middle-aged dame with eyebrows growing vertically; a sign of noble breeding.

Her meeting with The Ruler took place on a blue-sun day. They had an equal number of blue-sun days and yellow-moon days during each year of four hundred days; the Runa calendar, named after the daughter of Zika who had invented it. Sheets of rain fell during the moon days.

She neared the royal palace, which consisted of five bungalows around a central courtyard. The courtyard was paved in stones, polished with elephant blood. These stones emitted a greenish-red glow hovering at ankle length. Walking on it Artemis looked like a spectre gliding along. This effect was enhanced by the cape she wore in case of rain.

A popular leader, The Ruler did not have bodyguards. Artemis could walk right up to where Her Highness was dozing, on a bronze throne with carvings of a li-tiger baring its teeth on both sides of the wing-shaped back. The li-tiger had become extinct, following the route of the croc-snake, the finch-hyena and the egg-mouse. The leader reclined with her arms wide and her legs in a silent O, a gold crown dangling from one foot. Her slash eyebrows gave her, even in sleep, a look of perpetual surprise. On her lap sat a pet monkey, playing with her hair. It hid under the throne when Artemis approached.

Artemis coughed; The Ruler opened her eyes. They were pale, almost like milk. She glanced at Artemis, then away past her head. "You are my daughter's friend."

"The General? No. I haven't seen her for a long time." Artemis bit her lip. "We're not really friends. We just went to school together."

"If you see her, tell her to come home. I don't know why she left."

"I will. If I see her. Your Highness, I have something to report."

"Go ahead."

"I had a dream, a vision. I asked a shape-shifter to analyse it and it said…" Artemis realised that The Ruler may not like the criticism about their posture or their language. There were rumours that she banished dissenters to live in the forest. "Umm, it said that we needed to be rehabilitated."

"And you believed it?"

"Of course not."

"Then what are you doing here?" Still not looking at her, The Ruler twitched her eyebrows. That meant the interview was over. Artemis stood in front of her for about five minutes, hoping that she would say more, but she had closed her eyes, pretending to sleep.

Artemis left, forlorn. Where would she go now? She hated it when someone did not even bother to give you their attention when you spoke to them. The inhabitants of her homeland did that frequently, priding themselves on ignoring a person until they doubted their own existence; forming packs around a trend leader to exclude and victimise the less pretty, the too clever, and the different ones.

She went back to the shape-shifter to whom she had spoken earlier.

"I told you what the problem was," it said, impatient.

"But how do I fix it?"

"You'll know," it answered, leaving with such a loud bang that it stripped leaves from the trees. "Don't call me again."

By now Artemis was beyond frustrated. This wasn't good for her crabby disposition. As it disappeared, a leaf fluttered towards her. On the leaf, two words: The Rons. This was becoming too convoluted. She was furious.

The time had come to discuss it with Jessie, a friend to whom she had not spoken for a while because she had used her expensive perfume without asking. Jessie would know what to do; she knew everybody's business.

She'd been a pale child with jet black hair when she met Jessie. Afraid of crowds and public spaces, she would become increasingly agitated. If there was no relief she would start wailing uncontrollably. Make a scene, Ma said. There were only four people who could take her home: Ma, Father, and her two siblings, Janet and Micky.

At pre-school she'd temporarily been without support and, terrified, had begun mewling softly. Shadows of adults had moved in and out of her sight but none had come to her aid. Her terror was building when someone gently touched her face and lifted her chin. Jessie. "I'll take you home," she'd said. Artemis had looked at the slight figure the same age as her – four and a half – and asked, desperate: "Who are you?"

A confident child, Jessie had examined the picture of Artemis' family on a string around her neck. "I'm your family friend," she'd smiled. There was reassurance in that wide smile. It'd calmed her. Taking Artemis' hand, Jessie had led her home.

Ma was not pleased. "You're supposed to be in school." She'd glared at Jessie. Jessie had given her the same disarming smile. "I'm Jessie," she'd said, "and I have a gift for sick people." Ma was amused: "Really?" Jessie had nodded seriously. "I just knew she was sick and had to come home."

"It would appear that you've made a friend." Ma laughed the laugh that usually made Artemis curl up in a foetal position.

Jessie had indeed become her friend, her best friend, her only friend.

Father had died in an accident when Artemis was six. He'd been her primary caregiver. While driving to work he'd strayed into a truck. Her eldest sister, Janet, had been with him.

He had more patience, Ma said. He read to her and taught her how to control her fears by deep breathing and self-hypnosis, which could sometimes allay the onset of her symptoms, and sometimes not. Janet, much like him, had been a big sister who acted more like a little mother.

The loss of her father and sister had aggravated Artemis' condition. Ma and Micky were close and she the outsider. While grieving she'd realised, in that rare moment when one glimpsed truth sanctioned by the subconscious, that she was surrounded by people who only had contempt for her.

Under the shroud of a broken heart she'd laboured to build distance between her and her mother. Her detachment became a buffer against the wrenching pain that accompanied all interactions between them.

But she had inflicted a wound in her own being, a laceration between her thoughts and what she could feel in her body. Crippled thus, she was numb and couldn't feel her quickening heart rate and flush of anger, the sinking stomach of disappointment, even the flowering of love. That is, until she'd met the deer-man whom she had lost.

Wearily she went on another journey to find Jessie. Although she thought Jessie a bicycle, she had reached the end of her endurance. After six cycles of sun days and moon days she found her.

Artemis was standing on a shoebox balcony in a high-rise building of raw brick, her back to the rail, animatedly talking. She seldom sat down now because although she consciously stretched her legs out straight in front of her after the seer had interpreted her vision, they automatically flexed in unguarded moments.

Facing her, seated on a chair in the trademark posture was her best friend, Jessie, blonde, with insect legs and a rotund body. Wearing a pale pink pants suit, she had the air of a celebrity.

2.

You clicked your tongue and stormed out. Jessie laughed her head off and had to look for a substitute, which she kept in the bottom drawer of her closet, a face for each occasion. You were thinking embarking on this crusade would require you to give up a way of life, quiet and uneventful.

You knew that she wouldn't understand, yet you'd tried. She betrayed you once so why not again. You established that The Rons was not the place she had described. She just liked to yank your restraint.

Ma and Micky had not been any better. They'd left you in an asylum when in your intermediate years you had temporarily lost your way, two years after the deaths of Father and Janet. Jessie had left to live with her cousin in the city.

One morning, on a blue-sun day, you went into the kitchen and heard finch-hyena voices, high-pitched, laughing. You saw the outline of two animals approaching, with sloping backs and feathers. Their mouths were agape, revealing an acacia tree with delicate leaves and huge thorns growing horizontally. Mesmerised by fear, you cowered between the stove and the table the whole day and night. Someone had to come and lead you away. They never allowed you to forget that. In their eyes you were weak, had grown horns and a tail.

Ma preferred Micky, pretty, feminine, docile. Not you with your questions, saying odd things like 'If this is the way a girl is supposed to be, I don't want to be a girl'. Difficult child that you were, you grew into a troublesome teenager; too keen to point out injustice, perceived or real. Expecting justice where there should be none.

After your discharge from the mental hospital, you went home. They had turned your bedroom into a sewing room. Now you lived in a shed outside the kitchen door. Loving them had become challenging. It demanded so much forgiveness.

You were an imposter in your own life. You might as well have lived in the land of The Unknown, a barren place of harsh winds and snow, you'd heard.

You had watched the deer-men prancing in. You couldn't imagine the impact it would have on your lives. Usually they only came for the week-long Wassas festival, every alternate year. Now they were illegal residents, subduing everyone.

Your countrywomen were in awe. The invaders' strength and aggression intimidated them. The war-like deer-men had captured your world.

That day, that terrible day, you heard the ghosts bleed out of the women's bodies. Your own ghost tore from your frame causing unbearable pain. Shrieks of agony turned the yellow moon orange.

Losing an important part of your body and the consequence of your people's defeat made you feel empty and violated. And there wasn't even a confrontation, unless you counted shock and awe as a weapon.

Your ghost and the ghosts of the others have roamed the landscape since. Unstable, they changed into a man or a woman or a man-woman or elephants forming a protective circle around calves when the young bulls were in must. Taking on any form, they were the shape-shifters with no home to call their own.

Yet your own ghost visited you intermittently. You knew it was there, beside you, whenever you felt strong. You mourned its loss.

You pondered if it was profitable to close up all the holes in the women's bodies. Then they would have to come together to discuss the merits of each opening. An awareness of their body in the world would result.

But you didn't trust your own wisdom. You made bad decisions. You didn't need Jessie's company to fetch a child, yet you had invited her to the festival when you should've gone alone. Only you were selected that year, the year of the croc-snake, the last in a six-year cycle: gnat, li-tiger, egg-mouse, finch-hyena, elephant and croc-snake.

You had hoped for a little girl who could remain with you. The deer-men took all the boys to teach them deer skills. Running, jumping, fighting. A friend of yours, Mokki, had refused to give up her boy child. The deer-men came in formation, marched to her place, and dragged the boy away, kicking and screaming. You wanted a girl child. And Jessie, who could've had any deer-man she wanted, chose yours.

You were watching the mating dance of the deer-men. They had formed two lines with their antlers held high. You noticed that their white and tan hair lay flat on their bodies. Kick-kick, shuffle-shuffle. High jump. Forward, backward. Side to side. Their hooves, polished for the occasion, reflected the light from the blue haze of the fertility goddess, a statue of a mother and child. The air was filled with cologne from their musk glands situated under one of their back hooves.

Your eye fell on a tall one. His antlers had many branches. When he danced, his hind leg muscles rippled. You saw that he could probably run fast. He was so taken up by the movement that his loose lips peeled back to reveal the tough membrane of his top gums and uneven lower teeth. You were amused. Your eyes met and then he was dancing for you alone.

Later his loose lips fulfilled its promise of being a good kisser. Then Jessie appeared. She sat down at your table, uninvited, drinking, staring at him from under her lashes until he felt the heat of her gaze. Her unmistakable offering entrapped him. Glancing from a maybe to a sure thing, he was in a quandary. And then he was gone.

Amid the merriment you were sad. You had lost your suitor, your best friend and part of your motherland. You noticed that there were no flowers in the occupied territory. Then you remembered that the deer-men ate the grass, plants, flowers, buds, twigs, stems and the leaves. When food was scarce they ate the bark off the trees.

You knew that their newly developed antlers had velvety hair which they scraped off on the trees and branches when the antlers had grown to full size. They shed their antlers during the blue-sun days. You had seen these antlers scattered across the landscape, embedded in the soil, strange dried-up shapes, like sculptures.

You had to save your country from the destruction of the deer-men. The antlers decomposing in the sun caused vapours that had resulted in the gradual decline of births. You worried that soon it would cause the sterilisation of all women.

You had to forgive Jessie, even if you were reluctant. You could get musk for perfume from the muti killers, the deer entrepreneurs who robbed their colleagues of their glands under their hooves and inside their stomachs, leaving them split open, their intestines bubbling with green gnats.

A whisper went out from the manufacturers when musk was needed: 'A young stag, a fawn, or an older one'. This whisper was carried in the white dust until everyone knew. From then on they regarded each other with suspicion and fear. Those who qualified barricaded themselves in until several deer-men, the number specified by the multinational corporation, were found in the forest, disembowelled, their hind legs cut off. Only then the ones who hid came out to graze. Till the next time.

This happened twice a year.

If you got musk, your wealth would be diminished. It was prohibitive, but you had no heirs. Ma and Micky would have to work for their own support. You would save them from sitting in the sun the whole day; they had already acquired a blue tinge.

Nonetheless you should not alienate them. Your country needed you, but it also needed Ma, Micky, Jessie and all the other women. Without unity you were defenceless.

You called Jessie at home. She said that she was glad that you were friends again.

You hit the campaign trail, canvassing to win women to your cause. You heard pale women say they were oppressed. You heard dark women say they were oppressed. Yet they never made the link that they were oppressed together.

Raising your voice made you a shrew and caused fragile friendships to break in an instant. You mourned the fact that you were gladiators, women opposing each other, adversaries, competitors.

You persevered. With your new awareness, when women talked you listened by intuition and filling in the gaps; prodding for an inspiration, a way of approach.

Your hope was fading, but eventually every empire falls. However it commanded action. You remained lucid, thinking. It would require you to give up a way of life.

You looked around you and wished that your fellow countrywomen were not so jolly in captivity.

1.

I had collected my army. There were not as many heads as I had hoped, only four thousand. We started our basic training. Divided into three groups, short, medium and tall, the tall ones rode the elephants while the medium and short ones rode the monkeys and the birds, respectively.

Gold armour adorned the elephants, the boots of the ten wombmen on the backs of the giant animals, crusted with ivory spurs. The monkey and bird armour were light. They carried only one rider.

Weapons were in short supply. The manufacturers were still poring over designs for combat wear. It would be many moons before they were delivered. Meanwhile some had old guns, some rifles and some had swords. The mood was festive like a baby shower.

The General, Princess Alina, was in despair. I had to dig into my small repertoire of swear words to bring about a stiffer attitude in the recruits.

"Enough!" The General brandished a shotgun. "This isn't a picnic or whatever you miserable lot think it is. This is a matter of life and death. This is war!" She grabbed a sword and plunged it into the nearest trainee. Deathly silence reigned. "Now that I have your attention, drop! Crawl!"

I dropped to the ground, assumed the prone position, my legs jittery.

"Stop, look around you, listen for the presence of the enemy, smell before you move."

All I could smell was the white dust which had a cinnamon flavour. Crawling was excruciating. Not a position designed for those with breasts. We would've done better to crawl on our sides. Trying to keep my body flat against the earth, the uneven ground sheared my well-developed chest as I moved.

"Push your arms forward! Pull the leg on the side you hold your firearm. Forward! Now pull with your arms and push with your other leg. Keep the muzzle of your firearm off the ground. Look for your next position before leaving a position. Move!" The General kicked a cadet.

I winced at the yowl. Alina had no breasts, she had cut them off to improve her stealth in stalking an enemy.

My makeshift elbow and knee pads were in shreds. Blisters formed. The loose stones cut and bruised my skin. At least this was a cure for our sitting position, I consoled myself. Holding a weapon kept the arms busy, and crawling like a lizard straightened the legs. I could see muscles forming over my calves.

"Keep your mind on the battle! You're responsible for the safety of those around you. Who is the enemy? Say after me. The deer-men. Again, louder! The deer-men!"

We were taught to crawl, shoot, and to hate. The General was indefatigable. After basic training we were diverted into combat specialisation. Then we were ready.

Faced with the prospect of war, Jessie balked. "I can't do this. We are no better than them."

"So what do you suggest we do?" Uneasiness had settled in my stomach on the first day after the unnecessary death with the sword. Reality was harsher than the dream. Millennia of warfare had warped the deer-men. Conquer, rape, kill, pillage. A recipe handed down for generations. Coupled with periodic efforts at peace, it was unsustainable.

Jessie thought long and hard. "We could be a peacekeeping force. You can't fight fire with fire."

"Last time I heard, it worked," I mumbled.

"The most potent weapon of war is the mind of the oppressed. Steve Biko. We have to free our minds."

"Er... I don't know."

Jessie's words weighed on my mind. *The most potent weapon of war is the mind of the oppressed.* But what could we do to remedy conditioning that had endured for centuries?

Most of us concentrated on the emotions generated by what the deer-men said or did. On what made us happy, angry or sad. We seldom had an unfettered mind to think and strategise.

It was clear, only when our emotions were under control could we see The Path. Chained to the deer-men, we veered this way and that, never free, and not realising that we weren't free.

I decided to speak to The General, Princess Alina. Soft-spoken and charming, she had a character which belied her appearance.

I found her sharpening her knives. The shavings came off the tree branches in long, even curls until the edges were sharp. She tested one on her cheek. "We need a training exercise," she said when she saw me.

"Yeah." This wasn't going as I had hoped.

"I was thinking of going into The Unknown."

I tried not to show my fear. "Alright."

She called everyone and informed them of her decision. I could sense their uneasiness, but now that we were in a situation where the sharing of vulnerability could be interpreted as weakness, each one held their silence. "Yes, ma'am," they droned as one.

We hiked over mountains, lakes and rivers. Every night we camped in a donga or sloot and resumed marching the next day. After three weeks we came to the border, a hedge of almond trees.

Slowly we ventured into The Unknown. It was a black hole. Tall trees grew along the sides and bottom, bearing green hairy fruit the size of a fist. Giant crabs huddled under the trees, feasting on the fallen fruit. In the middle was a fire pit. Smoke and red flames licked the burning rocks. Viscous mud clung to our boots. Sitting on the fruit, buzzing around, were millions of fruit flies.

"Keep them away from me!" A deer-man jumped out, slapping wildly.

"Where did he come from?" I was puzzled.

"A stowaway." The General caught him by the hind leg. The fruit flies descended on him. At first he fought them off but then something strange happened. He became docile, gentle even.

"How can there be a stowaway, we only have our backpacks?" I said.

"I don't know how he got here, but he is a godsend. Good for our training."

"Training…" I was uneasy. The General fixed me with her milky eyes. I didn't like the expression in them. They were small, cold.

"The fruit flies seem to like his type." The General prodded him with a knife. In her mouth the sibilant sighs of our language became angry hisses.

"I can polish all your shields. I can carry your bags." He could sense that she wanted to kill him. Fruit flies dropped from his mouth as he spoke, from his nostrils.

The General stabbed his chest and flayed him open. He looked shocked, tried to close his chest flaps. She pinned each of his legs with a knife to the ground, leaving him spreadeagled.

"Hail, my queen," he said to everyone who had lined up under her orders to stab his heart to experience a kill.

I was third in line behind The General and Jessie. The blood gushing out of his heart excited me. Having never killed before, it was intoxicating. I longed to plunge my spear in more than once.

Long after he was dead and his heart had lost its shape to become a bloody mess, warriors walked forward, relishing in the task. The ones who had already stabbed him scooted to the back to rejoin the queue. They stabbed his body, his legs. They stabbed his antlers.

My blood had cooled. My sense of fairness, honed on being the last to be considered in our family, surfaced. There was a lot of us and only him. "Enough." I tried to stop the warriors. "Leave him now." They were blind with rage. The queue kept forming, reforming. Eventually I threw myself on the bloody corpse.

"Spoilsport."

"Whose side are you on?"

Their rage was palpable.

The General plucked me to my feet, pushed me into a tree. The green fruit smeared on the blood. She stepped forward, holding up her hands. The queue stopped. "Search and destroy," she spat the words out, furious eyes fastened on my face.

Whoops of joy accompanied the troops as they stabbed the trees and the fruit, the fruit flies, the crabs (who scuttled into the fire pit), chanting, singing 'One down, more to go'. The orgy of killing stretched into the night.

The next morning I was overcome by guilt and remorse. The General would discipline me. Of that I was sure. I had violated a direct order. Furthermore, I was mortified at taking part in such an unseemly massacre. That wasn't me, or was it? I was a soft-spoken, gentle person. Who would've thought that I had so much anger dammed up inside me? It was as if all the anger from my childhood till now had coalesced into a madness that scared me. I thought I knew myself but now I wasn't sure. Was that what war did to your psyche?

Remorse almost crippled me. Easily moved towards guilt by Ma and Micky, I had developed the habit of agonising over the tiniest detail. This was my fault. I had agitated for it. I had worked hard and had been proud of my accomplishment. Now I viewed the dark abyss of my regret. Should I abandon the project?

The next morning as I cleaned up the blood and debris (my punishment), I drafted a letter in my head to my colleagues: 'Dear Sisters, it has come to my attention... after much thought... I've come to the conclusion... should we reconsider... please bear with me... dear sister...'

I couldn't find the words. My passionate conviction that the Akerians should be free had not wavered. What I was struggling with was the how; how to achieve that freedom without bloodshed. I was seriously considering asking my comrades to pack up and go home. A movement in the corner of my eye – Jessie was quietly helping me.

"I think we should go home."

"What are you saying?"

"I made a mistake. All this blood..."

"We've come so far, and now you want us to turn back? Some things cannot be undone."

I watched the enthusiastic drilling of the troops and knew she was right. They had recovered from the previous night with bright eyes and even brighter smiles. The supplies had arrived. A new energy and sense of purpose accompanied each step. They were a cohesive force, a true army. "What have I done?"

"Pull yourself together. You can't allow them to see your doubt. This is a sacred war."

Yes, it was a sacred war, sanctioned by the years of oppression. Our freedom was finally within reach. A new world awaited; one without restrictions. We would be able to go to the shrine whenever we wanted. We would own the sacred rite of rebirth.

We were facing each other across the river, the deer-men proudly holding their heads erect to show off their crowns of antlers. The captain stepped forward. "Let's not do this," he said. "It'll be a massacre."

"Whaddaya mean?" Jessie danced in front of him, throwing mock punches.

"Do I know you? Haven't we met before?"

"No."

"Looky here, I sent the other troops home. We're professional soldiers. We want a worthy opponent. And frankly, this is..."

"What?" Jessie's punches whizzed past his nose.

"A joke. That's what it is. We outnumber you in strength, in experience, in every way. You ladies are gonna get a hurt."

That's when Jessie landed a punch. The captain staggered back, his antlers swinging from side to side, levering him off balance. A stone found his head. He dropped down, unconscious.

His army attacked. We fought like demons; Jessie in front, leading. The General sliced and diced with her knife. Millenia of frustration and anger had formed a pool of aggression to drink from. The older women had more anger than the younger ones. They celebrated the opportunity to harness this rage before they turned it in on themselves.

Soon the deer-men retreated, having underestimated their opponents, who gave chase, drunk with victory. "Go! Voetsek! Go, and never come back."

"See-ya at the Wassas festival," the deer-men whispered as they limped home.

"Let's go after them." Jessie wanted to follow the deer-men into their own territory, to rape and to pillage. She had become a fierce warrior.

"We can't do that," I said.

"Why on earth not? And we should take slaves and march them through the middle of Akere."

I indulged my mind in a dream of the deer-men, broken, shuffling along in chains, kicking each other's back legs for want of an enemy. But that wasn't what I wanted. I was having second thoughts about violent rebellion.

It was necessary but it had consequences. I had seen what it did to decent women, it coarsened their sensibilities. Once home they may not know the difference between state-sanctioned killing and personal killing, having lost the natural barrier not to kill their own kind.

And my foray into killing had left me troubled, rationalising the need for such action, but in conflict with my belief system 'Do unto others as you would like them do unto you'. Women like me couldn't be separated from their emotions, and it wasn't bad, just tricky. "I thought you were a pacifist."

"A person can change."

"The only reason we won here today is because they were arrogant."

Jessie pondered. "But what are we going to do next? Take over the world?"

I laughed, feeling free for the first time. "We could go home?"

"No, that's boring. We need another mission."

"Of course. But we'll have to discuss it with The General."

"She's cute. She has the most beautiful ears."

"I never noticed."

"They're delicate, like a seashell. And she smells good."

When the final column of deer-men crossed the border back into Mamela, the blue sun danced. It threw yellow and red streaks across the sky. A high wind came up. There were shrieks as the shape-shifters swooped back into their owner's bodies. Lightning flashed green. Black clouds bubbled. Everyone cheered.

My shape-shifter didn't immediately come into my body. Half of it was already there and it was quite a struggle to fit the two pieces together.

I had gained the other half during a return-to-life experience after an accident. I'd been painting the purple birds' nests when I fell out of a tree. I died: I saw a dark light and heard the opinions of my deceased relatives. To a woman they were saying, "Get shorty." Hours later I'd woken up with a devastating headache.

Since then, I'd been half-human and half-ghost. On the periphery of life, observing, but not quite a part of it. Penis envy hadn't entered even the remotest parts of my mind.

"We have a crisis." The General had a clipped way of speaking. "The shape-shifters of the dead are leaving!"

I couldn't understand her concern. "Is that bad?"

"They're holding back the sea!"

"Eh. I had forgotten. What are we going to do?"

"Ask my mother to help."

She started running. I followed. When we reached the palace, The Ruler was already waiting, holding the reins of an elephant. "Hop on," she said.

We raced back to the strip. The sea was already coming in. Soon there would be a tsunami.

"Do something." Even amidst the worse battles, I had not seen The General so agitated.

The Ruler waded into the sea. She held aloft a stick. "Whoa." The elephant stopped. She began speaking in a calm voice, explaining to the shape-shifters that they were needed there, at sea.

"We have to ask permission," one croaked. Slowly, taking turns, they disappeared into a mist which hung upon the sea, to visit the dead bodies of their owners. Very sad they came back, some of them sobbing wildly. Eventually they were all back and the sea receded.

On the way home, victors, Jessie came to hang on my shoulder. "You know, it's not our job to fix these deer-men. They must fix themselves."

"Amen, sister."

We continued walking. "I'm sorry I called you a bicycle. We shouldn't call each other names."

"That's fine, my friend."

"During this trip, we've become close again. I'm happy."

She tossed her hair. "I still think we should be like the purple birds!"

It occurred to me that I apologised too much. In all my relationships I was the one who made all the effort. I was attracted to people who pushed me away while I strived to get closer.

When we reached home, crowds lined the streets to cheer. Drums accompanied us and we sashayed in rhythm to the beat, swinging our hips, proud to be women. The apathy and hostility we had experienced before we left was gone. Placards read 'Akere for Akerians', 'The right to self-determination' and 'Woman's rights now or never'.

"Welcome home." Ma and Micky met me at the front door. They had moved their sewing room to the veranda and given me back my room.

"Are you hungry?" Ma said. "I made a steak and kidney pie." I was touched. We hugged, people who were not used to hugging, tense, awkward.

After dinner Micky watched while I unpacked, eyeing my tan, grey and green uniform with respect. "I wish I was more like you." That gave me pleasure. I smiled at her, my cheeks stiff at the unusual activity. We didn't have much in common. She was like Ma, a lady. I answered her questions about the war until she became sleepy.

Ma came into the room, carrying a cup of hot milk. Being welcomed back as a hero had made me mellow, softened my guard in her presence. And she was serving me, something she had not done in the past. I was always the one to serve her. "I'm sorry I couldn't be more like Micky." I looked up expectantly, trying that smile again.

"No need to apologise. You are not my child."

Shock. "Did I hear…you said…"

"Surely you must know. I thought you knew."

"No… I didn't."

"It's not a big deal. We can still live together. Carry on as before." She laughed. "Lots of people are not related."

"Does Micky know?"

"Yes."

"Who else… knows?"

"Oh, a lot of people, I didn't keep it a secret. The principal at your school, Jessie—"

"Jessie knew and she didn't tell me?"

"Don't be so melodramatic. She heard us talking one day."

I laughed bitterly. "So everyone knew except me." Against my will I started crying. "Is that why you locked me up and made me eat paper? I thought it was because I was not pretty like Micky. How could you treat me like that and not tell me why? Instead you told the whole neighbourhood."

"I'm not listening to this." She turned to leave. I grabbed her arm. "You will listen. By God, you will. If it's the last thing you do. If you move, I'm going to shoot you." I picked up my assault rifle.

She let out a yelp. I could see she was afraid. For once I was the one with the power. Not the helpless little girl that she beat with a tree branch. She used to prolong the punishment and my fear by asking me to go into the forest to cut a swish. "It's too thin," she would say, inspecting it, or, "It's too short." I was so angry my blood throbbed in my temples. I had to vent my anger or go mad. With tremendous effort I calmed down. "I won't hurt you." I breathed deeply.

"Get out." She spat the words into my face.

"I'll pack my stuff and leave tomorrow."

She ran from the room, leaving a wet spot on the carpet.

At last I fell into my own bed. I slept, undisturbed by dreams but troubled by the presence of all the deer-men I had killed. They would appear before me in their death pose, stiff with blood on their heads or necks where they had been shot, or with stab wounds, slit throats or visible intestines. My fragile mind struggled with this burden.

When doing mundane things like cleaning my new house or drinking tea, I suddenly saw in the middle of the bucket or cup an image of me stabbing or shooting. The desire to harm someone was overwhelming.

And then there was the fear of losing my mind again, which followed me around until I wanted to scream. But screaming would indicate the very thing I was trying to avoid – loss of my sanity, and a return to the mental hospital.

I realised that I would not recover. I faced a lifetime of trying to reconcile my previous principles with what I had become.

A week later The Ruler called a national indaba, a conference. My sisters trekked from far to attend. It was the biggest gathering in the history of our country. We discussed having a regular army and how to keep the deer-men from re-annexing the strip.

Focussed on restoring the ecology, we deliberated on the clearing up of the detritus of antlers, which required extensive work.

With the help of the fruit flies we hoped to maintain our sovereignty. In the laboratory it had been established that these flies were attracted to testosterone, which they gobbled up in gunks.

The Ruler planned to import them to release all over our land. But that would happen only after we had eradicated all the insect-eating plants.

WALKING SCHOOL

They met at walking school. An entrepreneur had seen a gap in the market: that someone should teach people how to walk.

In his thorough research he saw different kinds of walks, the flat-foot, the duck, the bounce, the toe, the heel; and the different ways of swinging arms, high, low, slow, fast, and the jumpy movements under the arms of those on drugs.

Said entrepreneur grasped that when we start out, stumbling across the floor in our first run-walk from one parent to the other, the parents are so happy. What an achievement, they've taught their offspring to walk!

All you get is extravagant praise, and shrieks of "She's walking!" Not a thought is given to technique.

Consequently, these unfortunate individuals have a walk that is a liability. In the duck walk, the feet face outward and the owner stabs sideways with his feet for the rest of his or her life. The heel walk has the individual slamming his heels into the pavement, wearing out his shoes.

If the feet are placed down flat on the ground, it creates a natural swing in the hips, the most attractive walk – in a woman, that is. A man could get away with lots of broad-shoulder arm swinging and nobody would even look at his feet.

Petra had a peculiar walk. She leaned forward, rowing with her feet in tiny steps, her head bobbing, sending her long plait which reached to her coccyx swinging from side to side. She wasn't pretty but she had large, mesmerising eyes to the side of her head like a horse. Black in colour, they looked out at the world in interest and wonder.

John was a side-walker, turning his feet on their sides to warp his shoes as they leaned like drunken sailors. He would've loved to have been a toe-walker, dancing on his five digits, light as a feather. But, alas, you seldom get what you desire.

He enrolled in the second semester.

He bumped into Petra on the stairs. Immediately he fathomed that a person who looked into her eyes, fell into them. And he wasn't an easy fall-into-eyes kind of person.

Impenetrable, her eyes never reflected her thoughts but rather reflected the glance back to looker, a most uncomfortable experience. But Johnny came, he met, he conquered.

They were married by the end of that year.

For ten years, they were happy but childless. They didn't want to go through tests to ascertain whose fault it was; they loved each other too much for that. They shared the blame, equally, bravely. They decided to adopt.

The first day they walked into the orphanage, they saw a laughing boy walking on his toes at such great speed that they had to jump out of the way. It was love at first sight.

The next day they learned that another couple was also interested in taking him home to embark on the long journey of raising a child.

How else to settle the dispute but with a walk-off?

A long table was found. On it they had to do three walks each.

FIVE

The children were not allowed to say that the adults became drunk, out of respect for their elders, so they referred to the people who came to the shebeen as happy.

The patrons talked and laughed, played music and danced. Held and kissed each other. It made the children happy, to see such happiness.

David thought how lucky he was to come from such a wonderful place. He had enough to eat, nice clothes and his own mobile phone.

David's friend at school was a quiet girl named Lindy. Lindy wore torn clothes and never smiled. David couldn't understand, because Lindy's father was one of the happiest men at the shebeen.

On a rainy Monday, Lindy came to school with the mark of a hand across her cheek. A purple-blue smear had grown under one eye. She walked in a funny way, as if riding an invisible horse.

David was curious. "What happened?" he asked. "One, two, three, four, five; five fingers, like our age!"

Lindy said that her father had hit her when he came home from the shebeen. She said that there wasn't enough money to buy food or milk for the baby.

David was uneasy when he saw the adults happy. He couldn't forget Lindy's sad way of walking.

He asked his ma about it. She introduced him to his sister.

AN IMPORTANT LETTER

Felicia sits at the kitchen table. She writes:

To Mom. Oh shoot, a red pen. Where's my black pen? It's not here in my bag. Did I leave it at school? No, I don't think so. But where could it be? I hate it when people take my things. Bruce. Of course, he took it. That brother of mine! I know I'm not supposed to say it, but he is a real pain in the butt. He's always taking my things. And then I have to look and look for it. Shucks. I hope Mom doesn't mind. This red pen is not an insult or anything, just that I can't find my other pen. Brother, I'm going to tell on you. This time you'll see. But Mom is busy with the wedding. I can't trouble her. She also doesn't listen. She's too busy cooking and baking for that Uncle Steven. I wish she would spend more time with me. Like she used to. But I have to concentrate on this letter. Look at my nails; I've chewed most of them off. The medicine Mom used to put on didn't help. In spite of it being so bitter. LOL. But that was before this special friend of hers came along. Now she hardly notices. So I can bite them as much as I want. Mm, my thumb… there's still a bit of nail there. Um-hum, I don't know why I do this. It doesn't even taste like anything. Hey, I have to write.

From Felicia. So far, so good. Now she'll know who the letter is from. But, what do I say, how do I ask? I don't want her to be angry. No. Then she'll say I'm just like my father. Or that I'm too big for my boots. I just want to be in the wedding, that's all. I would like to be a flower girl. Or maybe even a bridesmaid. I want to wear a new dress and flowers in my hair. Wow, wouldn't that be cool? The girls in my class will be green with envy. Quiet little Felicia, wallflower Felicia, is going to be a bridesmaid. That'll show them for ignoring me. The stupid cows. Can I help it if I'm clever and read a lot? They're so stupid and shallow. Enough of them. I have to write this letter. I hope it shows Mom that I support her decision to marry again, even if I don't. But we can't be selfish. She has her own life to live. Bruce says Uncle Steven is creepy. He ruffles Bruce's hair every time he walks past. Me, I stay far away from him. Now, what do I put in this letter? You know what, I'll just come out and say it. Be upfront.

I heard you are getting married, and I would like to be in the wedding. There, short and sweet. To the point. Daddy would be proud of me, if he ever came to visit. I wonder how I will recognise him. I was two when he left. But Mom says we have the same dark-brown eyes. So all I have to do is look into his eyes and I'll know it's him. Grandma says blood calls blood. I wonder if it's true. But it's time to end this letter.

Love. Oh wow. What am I doing? I just added my signature. It just happened. I've been practicing it for a while, on everything. Yesterday I signed on the kitchen table. Mom will have a fit. I have to clean it up. Mom doesn't know what my signature looks like. She's never seen it though I tried to show her. But there's never been a chance. How will she know it's my signature? I always get myself into these tangles because I don't think before I act. That's what Grandma says. I know, I'll just draw an arrow from my signature to my name. That'll fix it. Careful, now. Don't go over any of the words. But, now the arrow is crooked!

SAVING FACE

Her mobile phone buzzed. "Hello."

"Revenge," the person on the other side said in a deep voice.

"What... who?"

"I know how you can get back at them."

"Why are you disguising your voice, Judith? I haven't got time for rubbish."

"Aw, sorry. Remember I'm your best friend. Not that lying, cheating son of a …. Want to hear what I have to say?"

"Talk."

"I heard from a friend, a good friend, that that hussy, your husband's... uhm…"

"Yes?"

"I heard that she has four other elderly gentlemen."

"What?"

Judith laughed merrily. "She calls these gentle... er... idiots her ministers."

"I don't understand."

"Well, it works like this. Her Minister of Housing pays for her expensive flat, her Minister of Transport bought her a new car, her Minister of Travel and Tourism takes her on holidays and—"

"What is my husband's role?"

"Well, she's at university."

Silence followed.

"But don't worry with that, my sister, there's more. Her Minister of Finance is a well-known drug dealer."

Elizabeth started laughing uncontrollably, a mixture of hysteria and mirth. "Thanks, Jude. You just made my day."

Her husband, Robert, was on the front page of the Sunday Times newspaper. *Deputy Minister of Higher Education, Mr R Davids, and Mrs Davids at the Durban July, the biggest horse race in the country,* the caption read below the picture which was spread across the top half of the page. A smiling Robert, dressed in a silver suit, had his arm around a woman dressed in a shade of purple that matched his tie.

The woman at his side was about eighteen; the age of their daughter. A wide-brimmed hat almost obscured her face. Elizabeth looked closer. It was the cleaner's daughter. They had met briefly at his office and she had eyed Elizabeth with a glint in her eye as if she had summed up an opponent and found her wanting.

"Damn you!" she shouted to the empty house. Unchecked tears dripped down her face as she went into the kitchen. She flung open the cupboard where she kept the relics from their old life in a rural village ten years ago – paraffin lamps, candle holders, a heavy cast-iron pot – and found what she was looking for: an axe which they had used to chop wood. She carried the axe upstairs to their bedroom. Uttering a war cry, she plunged it into his bedside table.

Robert was doing what many of his peers did in government and industry in the new South Africa: rich, established, and previously poor men with money and power they were not used to, going out with young girls as a hobby; becoming sugar daddies, and adding to the spurt of Aids statistics among those over fifty.

As Deputy Director of Health in Limpopo, Elizabeth had gone to many conferences on HIV and Aids. At the last one, the lecturer had looked at the mostly older women present and said that the epidemic was fuelled by intergenerational dating. "Your husbands," she had said accusingly. "Where you're sitting now, you don't have your husband in your pocket."

Holding her upper arms, Elizabeth began to rock to soothe her-self. She was trembling. It wasn't happening, not to her. While all around them relationships had ruptured, theirs had stood strong. It had to, because she had put so much effort into it. She had sacri-ficed her career for ten years when the children were younger, at his request. Whatever Robert wanted, she was happy to give, even if she didn't agree; like growing her hair long when she liked it short.

She had come across a website once, sugar daddies looking for sugar babies. One entry had read, *Sugar daddy in a stable marriage with R6 000 a month to spend.* An answer: *Passionate and willing as long as the money keeps coming.* Transactional sex was driving a new economy. It wasn't prostitution, one sugar baby – a divorced mother – said.

Her stomach tied itself into knots. They were wearing her favou-rite colour. Suddenly dizzy, she put her hands on her head. How could he humiliate her like this? What would their friends say… and her mother? Her mother was sure to indulge in a maternal I-told-you-so; she had never liked Robert.

The telephone rang. Elizabeth considered not answering. It was Sunday morning and she was still in bed. It didn't stop ringing. With a sigh, she reached for the receiver.

"Did you see the newspaper?" Her mother.

"Yes."

"You should sue that paper. You should—"

"It's all good, Mother," Elizabeth interrupted. She didn't need this. Not now. "Don't worry. I'll deal with it."

She cut off her mother's reply in mid-sentence and placed the receiver next to the telephone so she couldn't call back.

He was a sugar daddy. Older men who, instead of addressing the gross disparity in income by assisting families who live on less than R1 000 a month, slept with their daughters as a generous gesture. Furtively, they bought clothes in women's stores in far-flung malls, and milkshakes for an eager face in school uniform bouncing excit-edly on the front seat of a convertible, while daddy leaned sideways to fish money out of his tight jeans.

She smoothed the crumpled newspaper, looked at the picture again, sobbing now. Her gaze fastened on Robert's bald, smiling image. He had taken to shaving off all his hair to hide the few bedraggled hairs that still grew on the back of his scalp like an apron.

Elizabeth remembered the insolent gaze of the young girl. After three children she had a thick waist and, at fifty-five, had acquired an internal heat source that burned her cheeks and caused her neck to sweat. Only this morning she had discovered a grey hair growing on the side of her chin. It was already the length of a fringe. Who had seen it before she did? she agonised. Was that why Robert was with a younger woman?

She heard his key turn in the front door. He was home. She wasn't ready to face him. Opening the doors of her built-in cupboard, she dived in.

She tried to pull the grey hair out by its roots. The hair lifted up the loose skin painfully, but held. For twenty years she had been a faithful wife, and now...

Heavy footsteps came up the stairs. She pictured him holding onto the rail to haul himself up, his stomach wrestling against his shirt. A thought came to her, a revelation. He was riddled with the side effects of Viagra. Dizziness, headache, flushing, blurred vision, excessive hunger. Yet they had not been intimate for six months. She had sensed his reluctance and didn't persevere.

"Lizzy!" He entered their bedroom, saw the newspaper on the bed, the axe.

"Jo-jo," she heard him say. He retraced his steps, almost running from the room.

If she wasn't so upset she would've laughed at the idea of him running, his stomach swinging from side to side. She crawled out and opened the window. The icy wind cooled her face as she watched Robert drive off.

Dishonour and hurt vied with the impending shame of having to face her colleagues; she would have to go for an Aids test.

The following Sunday the newspaper carried an apology because they had mistaken Mr Davids' employee for his wife. In a new photograph of Mr and Mrs Davids, Elizabeth had short hair in a bob. Two parallel lines scored the finger where her wedding ring used to be. Smooth, shiny baby skin showed between these lines; a fresh, permanent scar.

At the bottom of the page was a story about the arrest of a drug dealer. Mr Davids' cleaner's daughter looked dishevelled, trying to hide her face behind her jacket. All that could be seen was her expensive weave. No doubt purchased by the Minister of Hair.

THOUGHTS OF A SOLDIER

A battered diary was found among the rubble. On the top half of the first page, barely legible, was the inscription: Moses M. The bottom half of the page and a piece of the right corner had been torn out. Starting on the second page, the diary was filled with close writing that meandered across the lines, oblivious of the ordered spaces accorded to each day of the month.

'It is the year 1989 the 24ᵗʰ of December 1989 Soon we will enter a new millennium but there is no hope for the future I am 26 years old yet feel that I have lived too long I've seen so much blood too much blood The smell of blood seems to follow me like my shadow It is the third year of the war I had another nightmare Always the same dream I am in a narrow dark tunnel I'm stuck I can't get out I claw at the walls The tunnel starts collapsing I can't breathe I try to scream I wake up with my heart galloping painfully in my chest There is no hope that the war will end soon I'm sitting here on the bonnet of a burnt-out car It's covered in rust Writing with the short stub of my pencil I dread the time when it will be too short because I don't know where I will get another pencil It is New Year's Eve How I long for the times before the war When people still welcomed the new year with enthusiasm Now there is only despair When they decorated the outside of their houses with bright patterns When they made thick biscuits that looked like scones I long for the music from each house

For the picnic on New Year's Day I am alone now Yesterday I lost my friend He shouldn't have torn pages from my diary It isn't right My parents died long ago My brothers have been killed in this war I don't know what happened to my sisters It is a war we cannot win We have only AK-47s But we will not surrender Death before bondage We've given up too much already Our homes our lives our sanity At least the war gives us something to do Provides us with food in our stomachs Not like the women and children Our leaders in exile say we must fight to the bitter end I am so tired Will I ever reach the promised land Another attack This time I'm going to die My luck is running out No it's only the comrades celebrating the new year Shooting in the air and rattling empty tin cans I wonder what happened to Sara We used to go dancing on New Year's Eve Another year I cannot face another year Maybe the war will end soon Maybe our leaders will opt for peace No Freedom before serfdom Maybe Sara is in the refugee camps But maybe she is dead Mama Sara I AM COMING HOME'

I closed the diary slowly. The writing had only covered about ten pages, and suddenly I found the empty pages unbearable to look at.

THE RIGHT TO LIVE

A woman lies motionless on a bed. The room is furnished sparsely; an array of medicine bottles on a table, a urine bag on a chair. Her eyes are closed. A nasogastric tube protrudes from one nostril and bends across her cheek, where it is secured with pink plaster.

Her daughter, Thelma, appears; fortyish, obese. "The sister said you should listen to some music. To stimulate you to wake up." She switches on a small radio, puts it on the bed. Gospel music spills out, loud. She leaves.

The woman on the bed opens her eyes. They are opaque, the eyes of the terminally ill, as if they have a thickened lens. She can see, hear, feel and think. But, imprisoned by her body, she cannot move, talk or swallow.

In the kitchen Thelma prepares lunch. Her daughter helps.

"I wonder if your grandma will ever wake up again, Joanie. The stroke was bad, but she's been like this for six months now."

"Keep faith, Mom."

"She's fighting to live. I can tell. She's always been a fighter. And I can't wait for her to wake up. I miss her so much."

There is a knock on the door.

"Will the visitors never end?" Thelma says. "How many came today? Five? Six?"

An elderly woman is standing in the doorway.

"Hello, Mrs Baker. Please come in. My mother's in the room."

They walk towards the bedroom.

"Is she still…?"

"Yes, Mrs Baker, but don't worry. The sister said we must talk to her. Mummy, Mrs Baker came to see you."

The woman's breathing is laboured, tiny beads of sweat on her forehead. Her shoulder has fallen forward, obstructing her breathing.

"Come closer, Mrs Baker. Sit on this chair." Thelma hides the urine bag under the blanket.

Mrs Baker sits on the chair. "Hello, can you hear me? Mr Baker sends his regards." She takes the woman's hand in hers. "How long are you still going to be like this? You must fight the devil. He brought this illness to you. We're all praying for you."

Joanie comes in, sees her grandmother sweating. Instinctively she moves her shoulder, wipes her forehead and moves the pillow. The invalid sucks in a long, deep breath.

"Has the priest been here yet? Look, she's crying."

"No, Mrs Baker, she's not crying. Her tears just run down like that. Maybe to clean her eyes or something. I don't know. I don't know much about being unconscious."

The woman opens her eyes.

"She's looking at me." Mrs Baker moves back in the chair.

"I was also scared the first time she did that. Feels weird, doesn't it? But her eyes open and close all the time."

Mrs Baker leaves.

Thelma checks under the blanket. It is wet. The urine bag has leaked. They change the sheets.

"I know the sister said we must move Mummy every two hours, but it's not practical. Just not practical. I mean, I'm working full-time, plus cooking and cleaning. And taking care of her. Not practical."

Thelma throws brown fluid into a 50 ml syringe connected to the nasogastric tube. It's one of the concoctions left by well-meaning neighbours. The fluid moves backward and forward in the tube, in sync with her mother's breaths.

The bedridden woman's head moves back. Thelma jumps.

"Joanie!"

Joanie rushes in. "What's wrong?"

"Granny. She moved!"

The woman moves her head again.

"Thank God. She's awake." But Joanie keeps her distance, suddenly afraid.

"Maybe she's just having a fit," Thelma says. "Mummy!"

The woman moves her head a third time.

Thelma strokes her hair. "It is a fit. Shame, she's suffered so much. Maybe it would be better if she…"

Joanie holds her grandmother's hand, crying. "For a minute I thought she was coming back to us."

LAST WILL

1. Singing: 'Kay sera sera. Whatever will be will be. The future's not ours to see. Kay sera sera.'
2. I come from a small place in the Northern Cape and end here. My mother cut me out in the pattern of the May family.
3. Don't make biltong of me. I don't want to be at the mortuary for longer than three to four days.
4. I want my funeral to be on a Wednesday. That way you avoid the crowds, and those who want to come will take off from work.
5. I don't want people to say what a good person I was after I'm dead. Stop them, or chase them away. Or I'll get out of my coffin and slap them.
6. These doctors, they don't have work for their hands. They opened me up to look at my growth. They gave it oxygen; now it's going to outlive me.
7. If you say that is not so, how come it started growing faster after they opened me up? It's blocking my insides.
8. Tell the truth and shame the devil.
9. Don't waste your time with revenge. God comes on a bicycle; he takes his time, but he will get to you.
10. Use that picture of me in my grey suit for the funeral pamphlet. I always wore it for special functions at the church, like

when the bishop came. I look good in it. And remember to brush my hair.

11. Don't make a big deal out of straight hair. Dogs shit straight hair. But if you do have coarse hair, shave the peppercorns sitting on the stoep at the base of the head.

12. Place a glass over the coffin. I don't want people touching my face with their grubby hands.

13. This is the number of the people who can cook for the funeral. They make delicious curry. But you must watch them, they will want to increase the price. Don't forget. Watch them because when they come the night before to peel the vegetables, they come with big bags.

14. Always eat before going to a party. You don't want to be too hungry when you get there. And leave something on the plate.

15. Don't allow my sister to take over the funeral. She is full of herself and likes to be seen.

16. If you go out on the town the previous night, go to church the next day. You need it to make up for what you did.

17. Water my plants. I don't want them to die. And look after my garden. Planting flowers in the shape of a diamond is hard work.

18. Don't go and visit your neighbour when you haven't even emptied your pee pot.

19. I don't want anyone to faint and threaten to fall into my grave. My sister's child likes to do that. That is just foolishness.

20. Always wear clean underwear and mend the holes in case you faint. If money is tight, make panties from mealie meal sacks.

21. I want to lie on top of your father. When I met him at the station, he said, "That's my wife." We came to Johannesburg and started a life together. He was like a pattern that you cut out and fit to your body with pins.

22. But they buried him upside down and I don't want to be so untidy in death. Put me facing the right way. PS I just realised that I'll smell his feet.

23. I brought eleven children into the world and I expect all of you to contribute to the funeral. If you don't have the money, you can take out a loan. Don't be a holhanger.
24. Fight your children's battles. If you don't, who will?
25. Eat what you have. Once you've eaten, nobody can see what's in your stomach.
26. Never leave your girl child alone with a man.
27. Don't sleep until the sun has baked your behind. Get up early.
28. Clean on New Year's Eve. You don't want to go into the new year with the old year's dirt.
29. Don't be lazy; bake tarts and make ginger beer for New Year. Make pickled fish for Good Friday.
30. I wanted flowers while I was alive.
31. Be humble. Nothing will fall off from you if you are.
32. You can stand on your head and blow 'God Save the Queen' with your bottom and I still won't have another operation.
33. You can buy that concentrated juice. Make it in a big drum. That way it's cheaper.
34. Don't chase away anyone who comes to queue for food. Sometimes it's the only decent meal they have for weeks. God can come as a beggar, and then you've turned Him away.
35. Wash before going to the shop. Nobody wants to see your dirty face.
36. Open all the windows every morning to get fresh air.
37. You don't leave the grave until all the sand is in. People are so rude these days, leaving when the coffin is still open, standing around talking in their sunglasses.
38. If you are angry, go into a room and scream. It will make you feel better.
39. I have big pots for the funeral. I don't want people carrying away food when they take their pots. Aunty Marie likes to do that.
40. Ask the church for big bowls to make the salad in.

41. It's ok if you are black like a pot's bottom. As long as you have manners.
42. The priest will choose a time. I won't have to tell you this if you go to church regularly, but although I brought you up in the church, you have exempted yourselves from going to church.
43. I don't want to be prayed alive, so don't have a service for me every night:
    (a) People use up all the tea and you have to bake biscuits,
    (b) It is an excuse for drunken singing and crying.
44. Life is unpredictable. Never say 'little fountain I'll never drink from you again'.
45. Tell my grandchildren I love them. I know I'm not supposed to say it, but I'm going to die.
46. Ask Ouma Jemmins to wash my body if she's still alive. She brought all of you into this world and there isn't a better mid-wife for miles around. I remember her massages when I still worked at the dressmaking factory.
47. July is my son. I want him to be a pall-bearer. His father died at eleven and he had to work as a gardener. I've encouraged him to finish school. He's a teacher now. I'm so proud.
48. Take just what you bought for me. That will teach the ones who never gave me anything.
49. Don't fight at my funeral. I'll get out of my coffin and…
50. I have chosen the hymns. Don't stretch out the hymns. That is unnecessary. And Aunty Marie sings false.
51. I wish I could talk to you about dying. Such a lonely business.
52. Don't cry too much.
53. Now that I think about it, the dying is not the problem; not coming back is.

THIRST

Maria, a well-dressed young woman, is testifying before the Truth and Reconciliation Commission. She's wearing a hat with a veil.

Her interrogator, a man, asks her details for the record: age thirty; level of education, PhD; occupation, CEO of her own company which makes and sells hats; part-time poet. She's currently canvassing to be a ward councillor in Alexandra, Johannesburg. Marital status, single mother raising a small boy.

He asks about the incident, where it happened and when.

Maria: "It happened during a march." She pauses; her mind veers off, soars to look at what happened from above.

"I was in a hospital bed, a splint on my arm to secure the needle of the intravenous fluid running into me.

"Strapped to the bed, my body was motionless, my arm swelling because of fluid leaking from a broken vein. There was numbness, pain, and pressure from the bandages securing the splint. My bladder was filled to capacity.

"Drip-drip, one drop dragged the other down as it sheared off into the receptacle, the head of the plastic snake that led from the bag of fluid to my vein. There was a burning feeling where it met the warmer temperature of my body, filling it to capacity.

"I coughed. Up came wet frothy mucus, pinkish, flooding my lungs. I was drowning."

She stops, sees men and women marching, singing, toyi-toying. Banners and placards indicate that it is a march for women's rights. Briefly, she focusses on a young man.

The interrogator asks Maria if she knew the perpetrator. She says yes, he was a friend of the struggle. Her composure starts to slip. She sees flashbacks to a brutal rape; a necklace of fire.

"I was in a desert, the sun beating down on my head. My tongue was dry, cracked. I craved water. I was overheating. My body, my throat, was parched. Every cell in my body was dry, wrung out like a washcloth.

"I was dying of thirst, my tongue coated, stuck to the roof of my mouth."

A man is testifying. He states his personal details: age twenty-six; happily married; children, two daughters, six and eight. He says it was an act of war. Witness what happened in Bosnia. He pleads that he has remorse now and should therefore be forgiven. If he goes to jail, his family will lose a breadwinner.

During the silence that follows, Maria removes her hat, revealing a hideous burn. She digs in her bag, takes out a beret, fixes it on her head, and walks out, proud. She turns back to stand in front of her tormentor. Handing him the hat with the veil, she says, "Give this to your wife."

HOME SWEET HOME

The sound of the key in the door made her move the brush faster. With a practised twist, she piled her braids on top of her head, securing them with a hairpin. Her mouth held the five pins to follow. Always five.

"I'll be down in a moment, Ja-sy." Speaking around the pins, lips clamped to leave a slight opening.

Footsteps came up the stairs. They were different, heavier, more measured. She recalled the energetic running of his youth, smiled at the mirror. Hair done, she smoothed her dress, laughed spontaneously. Of course he wouldn't wait. He was full of life and ready to see her at once. She couldn't wait to see him too.

He appeared beside her reflection, taller, wider than she remembered; dressed in a dark coat and hat. When did he start wearing a hat, it was so...

"Hello, Mother." His voice had changed too. It was deeper. The war had made a man of him, but he was still her sweet child, wouldn't harm a fly.

"Jason, my son." She hugged him, waiting for the kiss on her cheek, leaned in, met his teeth on her cheek; an accident.

His eyes looked serious. Frown lines, deeper than they should be. She smoothed the lines with her forefinger, laughed again.

"I made meatloaf. With boiled egg inside, just the way you like it. And gravy. And mash." A feast for his homecoming. She had used her bus fare for the week, but she would walk from Johannesburg to Cape Town for the joy of having her son home again.

"I'm not hungry."

She looked up at him. His left sleeve was empty. Such a practical joker; she won't respond.

"Don't worry. We can eat whenever you're ready. I'll just put it back on the stove and—"

"I said I'm not hungry."

Her hand on the pot lid, she breathed deeply. "Ja-sy, there's no need to shout. Think about the neighbours. Everything is fine now. You are home."

"Do you call this a home? This mokhukhu?" He kicked a chair, the table leg. "Still satisfied with crumbs, are you? No wonder they could rule for so long, because of stupid yes-men like you and my father."

Pleading. "Ja-sy... no."

"Thank God you had us – the young ones – to fight, to save this country."

"Yes. You are a hero." She tried to touch his shoulder; he moved away. "Daddy told everyone how proud he—"

"Don't patronise me. What do I care what that old-timer has to say?"

"Please don't talk like that."

"Things are going to change around here. I need a beer; go get me a beer."

What had happened to her son? "I don't have any money. I used it to buy this. Mince for the meatloaf and—"

He swiped the pot from the stove. It clattered on the floor, disgorging mangled meat. A boiled egg, resembling an eye, rolled away.

Hiding her tears, she bent down. "I can pick the food up from the floor, don't worry."

"Get up." He yanked her to her feet.

She tried to smile. "I'm so glad you're home. Daddy will be pleased."

His fist to her temple, it hurt. "Don't lift your hand to your mother, it will fall off. Remember what I taught you. Oh God, no!"

"There's more where that came from."

Tears broke from her lids. "What's wrong with you?"

"You left the revolution to us, while you were bowing and scraping. And we paid dearly. We should've been in school…"

"I'm sorry." She started sobbing.

"Sorry won't give me back my arm. Or my life."

"Where's your other arm? I thought you were just hiding it from me, as a prank. No, no, don't hit me again. Please. I'm bleeding from my mouth, silly me, but don't worry, I know you're just tired. Aunty Dora's son, Jim, also came back like this."

THE OLD SUITCASE

Cedric was surprised at his strange feeling towards the unknown woman in the photograph. He had never seen her before, yet felt that he knew her, recognised her features. He held out his hands with the same reverence he had when he received his first communion. "May I touch it, please?"

"Sure." Gesina passed the locket to him.

He wrestled with the impulse to kiss the photograph, if only to make up for the pain the mysterious woman had suffered. Hastily, he handed it back, to avoid doing something stupid.

The Bible was the same size as Neil's grade one suitcase. It was heavy; he had to lean back, widen his stance. Laughing, he hugged the Bible to his chest. "I like the story about Castina."

Gesina nodded. "I'm glad. But it's not Castina, it's Ouma Castina. She's not your playmate. Where are your manners?"

"Sorry, Ouma."

"I want to ask you a special favour."

"Of course."

"Will you look after the locket and the Bible for me when I'm gone?"

"Me?" Cedric was overwhelmed. He was only eleven years old.

"Yes. You're my eldest grandchild. It must go to you. And you must pass it on to your children."

"Cool."

"Let's put it away now. Time for baby Ellen's bath."

Reluctantly, Cedric handed over the Bible. It had been like hugging the past, which stretched far back into a grey distance, beyond his life, and it'd been good. When he got up this morning he was just Cedric, son of Charles and Gloria Van der Walt. He had two grandmothers and one grandfather. Now he had a great-great (he didn't know how many greats) grandmother and he had been entrusted with the sacred task of looking after her Bible. His heart swelled with pride.

When Gesina came into the bedroom, Gloria had the baby to her breast. "You shouldn't feed her all the time," Gesina said. "She should get used to waiting. Otherwise she'll just cry at the first sign of hunger. And when the famine comes, she'll be the first to go."

Gloria clicked her tongue, pulled her nipple out of the searching mouth. Ellen whimpered.

Gesina kicked off her black slippers; the heel part was tramped flat against the sole, and shiny with wear. Each slipper had a ragged hole which matched the shape of the corns on her little toes. She was dressed in a housecoat. Buttoned down the front, she wore it like a dress over her petticoat.

Struggling to stay calm, she loosened and resettled her false teeth with her tongue, filled the bath, placed her granddaughter on her lap, undressed her and washed her. She dried her and liberally applied a warmed mixture of Dutch medicine: soet olie, rooilavental, stuip druppels and duiwelsdrek. The pungent smell permeated the room.

Gloria wrinkled her nose. "Is that really necessary? I bought baby oil and baby powder."

"But this is good for her skin. I used it on you and look what lovely skin you have." Gesina's eyes pleaded. "You just mix..." Her store of knowledge bubbled up, asking to be repeated. Acquired from her mother, who had acquired it from her mother, it was sacred. But Gloria frowned, waved away the strong odour.

Gently Gesina exercised the tiny arms and legs. She tied a flannel band, which she had sewn during the antenatal preparation, around Ellen's midriff, covering her navel with an old penny to stop a wind from coming in and forming a hernia. She anointed Ellen's head with castor oil, to prevent a blocked nose. Gloria sighed dramatically, rolling her eyes.

Gesina put the vest on inside out and brushed the fine, downy hair. She replaced the pendant of garlic cloves sewn into a small bag.

"Let me guess. That's to ward off evil spirits, right?" Gloria said, one side of her mouth drooping.

Later, Gesina was seated on a long bench in the medical outpatients department of Coronation, a 600-bed general hospital. Dressed in a black skirt and warm jersey, she wore her only pair of good shoes, black pumps worn at the heel. She came from a generation of women who lived in their housecoats and slippers, and was uncomfortable when dressed to go out.

She bit on her teeth, but not too hard; she was afraid of breaking them. Bought with her husband's small pension pay-out, they were irreplaceable. Her thoughts were on that morning. Gloria hadn't said thank you for bathing Ellen. The size 9 knitting needles clicked busily. Gesina's hands didn't match her petite frame. Broadened by hard work, her palms had deposits of callused skin at the base of each finger.

Next to her was a tall Indian woman. The government had decreed that these two racially classified groups may share the hospital, which was staffed mostly by white doctors who received an extra grant for working in a non-white area. The rest were Indian; black and brown doctors being scarce.

"The queue. It's not long today," the Indian woman said.

Gesina didn't look up from her knitting. "That's good," she answered. She didn't know the woman but it was normal to have conversations with strangers sharing the common goal of waiting to see the doctor. "Last time I was here it went all the way down the corridor."

She spoke Afrikaans, pronouncing her 'r' in such a way that it came out as a guttural 'gr'.

The woman touched the end of her knitting needle. "What you making?"

"Booties. For my granddaughter. She's getting baptised next week." Click-click went the knitting needles.

"It's a nice pink."

"Yes." Gesina contemplated telling the woman that she believed in a bit of colour. Although the booties didn't match Ellen's white dress for the christening, she had decided to make them anyway. Besides, it would be hidden under Ellen's long dress. And every baby girl should have a pair of pink booties.

Gesina's thoughts wandered to her conversation with Gloria about bus fare to the hospital.

"Did you speak to Charles?" she'd asked tentatively.

"About?"

"You know what I'm talking about."

"No, I didn't have a chance. I'll try and speak to him tonight." Gloria had been sullen.

"Thank you."

Anger flushed Gesina's cheeks. The indignity of a parent having to ask a child; and noticing that child's increasing irritation and erosion of respect. She'd frowned at Gloria, who had been a beautiful child. In a country that valued light skin, she had smooth pale skin and brown hair. The people in the village had asked, 'How can such a dark-skinned person like yourself have such a fair child?' To which Gesina had replied that a black hen also laid white eggs.

As she grew older she realised that she was not treated with respect. It was insidious and crept upon her almost unnoticed. One person showed disrespect and, if she didn't fight it, others started being disrespectful too.

"Do you come here often?" The Indian woman tried to bridge the silence.

"Once a month."

"Me too. I have high blood. The doctor says my blood pressure is so high it damaged my kidneys. I have to take tablets to wee otherwise I swell up like a balloon. My feet get so bad they don't fit into my shoes. When I poke my leg, like this," she demonstrated, "it leaves a hole."

Gesina stopped to stare at the dent in awe. She resumed her knitting, almost guilty about not having a more spectacular ailment.

"You're lucky. At our age your health is so precious."

Gesina nodded in agreement.

"Would you like one?" A samosa appeared in Gesina's line of vision.

"No, thank you," Gesina said politely. She had a bread and butter sandwich in her handbag. Most of the people in the queue had brought something to eat.

Following a well-worn groove, Gesina's thoughts returned to her struggles with Gloria. She hated living with her. Look what happened a week ago when Gloria had asked her to fetch the children.

She'd walked slowly, one hand supporting her knee, to the house at the end of the street where Cedric and his younger brother Neil were playing. She'd stopped near the gate, reluctant to go further. She didn't know the people, and they probably spoke English, a language she viewed with great fear because of her inability to speak it. She'd inspected her faded blue housecoat and tatty slippers; she wasn't properly dressed either.

She wore a headscarf. Underneath it she had numerous plaits with strips of pantyhose tied to the ends. These plaits came out of her head like Medusa's crown of snakes. In an era where women carefully styled their hair (chemically straightened and hair-sprayed into place), her scarf betrayed her as someone with one foot in the bush. But her plaits said here was a backward person with two feet firmly planted in a forest.

Thornton, where they lived, had been proclaimed as an area where brown people could live, and its residents were proud of its middle-class status.

Gesina had craned her neck to see if her petticoat was peeping out at the back. She'd grabbed it through her clothes and pulled it up, just in case. She'd straightened her scarf. "Waas julle!" she'd called. Where are you?

She didn't like the polite reserve of the people who lived there, she'd thought, leaning over the gate. You couldn't tell if someone approved of you or not. "Is iemand by die huis!" Anyone at home? She'd seen the lace curtain stirring. Putting one foot on top of the other, just one corn peeped out. She waited. The door remained closed.

"Coo-eeee!" she'd shouted. The dogs had started barking, first one then the other, until there was quite a commotion in the street. A black Alsatian had jumped over the fence about two doors down and it charged at her, swerved, charged again, slowly waving its tail.

"Voetsek!" Go away. Quite a few lace curtains were stirring by now.

Charles had come out onto the street, directed an angry glance in her direction, opened the gate and marched to the front door. She'd almost stumbled to get out of his way. He'd knocked, the door opened. Briefly, he'd said something which Gesina couldn't hear. The children had appeared. Ignoring her, he'd walked past, flanked by the two boys whose hands he'd held in an iron grip. Gesina had trailed in his wake, irritated.

There was movement at the beginning of the queue. Someone had gone in to see the doctor and the person next in line had shifted up one space. Everyone moved up one space, an undulating snake, swallowing up time. Gesina moved without interrupting her knitting. She still had a long wait.

"How old is your granddaughter?" the woman asked.

"Three weeks." Gesina smiled proudly.

"My granddaughter is a year old now. I have a picture of her here in my bag." The woman looked for the picture, produced it with glee. "Isn't she cute?"

"Hmn," Gesina said, not committing to a yes or a no. She thought it was the ugliest baby she had ever seen. A thin girl with a shaven head and bowl ears decorated by gold studs stared gloomily from the picture. Her dark eyes were ringed by black kohl.

Gesina's thoughts veered off again. Now, take that ugly dressing table. If Charles' mother had memories attached to it, why didn't she keep it? Instead she had given the bad luck of the cracked mirror to Gloria. And they were always visiting.

"When are they coming?" she'd asked.

"This evening. Charles told me last night."

"Can't they tell you a week before the time, like normal people? You could've invited your brother Eric. And I heard what she said the last time she was here. That you shouldn't stay in bed after having a baby, that it's old-fashioned. If she's so advanced why doesn't she take back her dressing table?"

"Ag, Ma." Gloria had shrugged, sounding tired.

The old man was okay but that old mare. Gesina grinned wickedly. Mrs Van der Walt Senior didn't have manners, and she wasted food. She'd not eaten that extra potato she'd taken; a mortal sin.

The queue moved again. The Indian woman kept up a steady stream of questions and comments. They didn't ask for each other's names. Gesina just answered questions and only occasionally made a comment. Eventually they were nearing the front of the queue. Their conversation slowed and naturally died down.

Gesina finished the row she was knitting, rolled the half-finished bootie around the needles. Knitting kept her fingers supple. Otherwise they became stiff and difficult to move. She put her knitting into a plastic bag, put the plastic bag in her handbag, an old scuffed leather trap. She fingered the sandwich in her bag, but decided to eat later. There were germs floating around. She could wait. When the famine came, she would not be the first to die.

She folded her arms across her chest, leaned back against the wall, and planned what to say to the doctor. Her arthritis was worse? No, she didn't want him tampering with her treatment, even though her middle finger had bent at the first joint like a root seeking water. She would say she just came for her tablets. That way, the consultation would be shorter and she could concentrate on asking for an extra container of wintergreen ointment.

Gesina's turn came. She got up from the bench, checked to see if there was any dirt or loose threads on the back of her skirt. Shining the benches damaged the fabric of your clothes. She straightened her jersey, which she'd knitted last summer. It had a collar and two pockets on the sides.

She entered the examination room. An Indian doctor was seated behind the desk. It was the young one. Still wet behind his ears, he was far too eager to change people's medications. But that was what happened when you were young. You thought you owned the world…

He looked at her file. "Mrs Kerspuy?"

"Yes." Gesina sat down on the chair opposite him.

"What can I do for you today?"

"I just came for my medicine."

He examined the file again. "Right. You have arthritis. Can you please go into the cubicle and undress? I'd like to examine you. Listen to your heart."

"There's nothing wrong with my heart. I only have arthritis."

"How is your arthritis?"

"Fine."

"Show me your fingers." He examined them one by one, moving each joint. Probably didn't have enough toys while growing up, Gesina thought. "Does it hurt?"

She winced. "No."

He put his stethoscope arms into his ears and examined her where she sat, lifting up her jersey. Gesina meekly obeyed his request to breathe in and out. He listened for a long time. Eventually he said there was a murmur, a sound that shouldn't be there. She would have to take new medication to prevent swelling. Gesina remembered the indentation in the leg of the woman in the queue.

He scribbled on the prescription page. "Anything else?"

"No, Doctor," Gesina said stiffly.

"Ok." He handed her the prescription.

She wasn't ready to leave. "There is something else."

He looked at her questioningly.

"Sometimes I'm unable to come to the hospital." She swallowed heavily, her pride buckling. "I need more wintergreen."

He scratched his head with his pen. "Okay." He added x 2 next to one of his scribbles.

"Thank you."

"No problem."

Gesina got up to leave.

"Next," he called.

When Gesina got home, she knelt with difficulty, pulled the suitcase from under her bed. She hadn't told the doctor about her excessive thirst and frequent visits to the toilet to pass water. She swiped the dust from the top. In a flash Cedric was at her side, helping her to lift it and place it on the bed. It was old and battered. Gesina put a gnarled hand on it.

Her whole life had been spent in anticipation of a famine that never came. She had a vague recollection of famine when she was about eight, when being able to withstand hunger was an asset. The red locusts had come to the small town in the south-western Free State where she had grown up, and destroyed the maize crop. Weak with hunger, she had to stand with her arms wide to catch the locusts and stack them into an empty maize sack; valuable food to be eaten later. Although she had a scarf around her face at the time, she experienced the sensation of the locusts beating against the cloth, sitting on her, and disintegrating in a slippery mess under her bare feet. But the most striking memory was that of almost suffocating to collect this flying food.

"I want to tell you a story. Listen carefully, because it is the story about your past. Once upon a time three ships came to South Africa. They came from the Netherlands, a faraway place across the waters.

The reason why they came was to create a halfway at the Cape of Good Hope. After that many people came to South Africa.

"One man, I forget his name, came from Holland. He had a daughter named Castina. She was beautiful with long, blonde hair that came to her waist. Her mother died when she was thirteen and her father married again. Her stepmother didn't like her at all, and when her father died, the stepmother, a Boer woman, started treating her badly.

"They had this big old trunk that they had brought with them on the ship. She would open it, put Castina's long hair into it and then lock it. Castina couldn't move. She would cry and try to pull out her hair, but she couldn't. Clumps of hair would fall out as she tried to free herself.

"Then her stepmother bought a slave from Madagascar. He, too, came on a ship. He was a musician. He fell in love with Castina. One day he stole the keys and unlocked the trunk. He freed Castina and they ran away."

Gesina opened her suitcase and took out an old gold locket, roughly made. It was oval in shape. A picture had been cut out and glued into the middle of it. Another picture, of a man, indistinct with blackness, was pasted on the back. The top of the locket was decorated with two spirals extending halfway down the sides. A gold ball on top had a small ring fixed to it, through which one could thread a chain. The picture in front was of a white woman in her early thirties, slightly plump, with her head turned sideways, looking wistfully at something or someone. "Here's a picture of Ouma Castina."

"Here's her Bible." Gesina took out a heavy book. It was black with brownish, well-used pages. She opened the Bible; the front inside cover was brown. In big font, *Bijbel* was followed by the words (in Dutch) *dat is de ganshe heilige schrift, vervattende al de kanonijke boek des ouden en nieuwen testaments. Door last van de hoog-mog, heeren Staten-Generaal der Vereenigde Nederlanden.* The published date was 1887.

On a yellowed loose page inside the Bible, handwritten entries were made of Castina's birth – 20 July 1874 – followed by the birth-dates of her ten children. Their names had been torn out.

"Here's a piece of her wedding dress." Preserved inside the pages was a small piece of stained netting.

Gesina didn't know the names of her other family members. Castina's light-skinned children had been assimilated into the white community while the darker ones had been cast out.

All she had was a story. Even this was unusual. Brown people rarely told stories about their past. It was shrouded in secrecy.

For the first time, Cedric was happy about his grandmother living with them. Although there was another bedroom, his father had changed it into his study. She shared the children's room. Her moving in meant that he and Neil couldn't jump on the beds or play Spiderman climbing down from the top bunk. They couldn't leave their toys on the floor, in case Ouma tripped over them. They were not allowed, under punishment of death, to touch her suitcase.

And then there was the problem of her teeth, which she took out at night and put in a glass of water on a chair next to her bed. There was a small radio on the chair too. While she was snoring, the teeth floated in the glass, smiling at him each time he happened to look at it.

But she wasn't all bad. On rainy days she made what she called oliebollen, with yeast and raisins. She fried it in oil until golden brown and sprinkled it with icing sugar. It was delicious. He had not eaten it anywhere else, not at the shops and not in his other grand-mother's house.

She said that it was a recipe handed down from her mother, who had received it from her mother. She in turn planned to hand it over to his mother. All this talk about generations bored him, but he loved the oliebollen. It couldn't help that it was weighed down with heavy talk. She had intruded, but now things were different.

There was a knock on the door. Probably his mother bringing cocoa, he thought. But when the door opened, his grandmother walked in. Cedric turned his face to the wall.

"Cedric?" He and Neil regularly made fun of her pronunciation of 'r', but at the moment it wasn't particularly funny.

"Yes, Ouma," he answered, although he didn't really want to. He was slightly afraid of her. She could get quite fierce.

"I want to talk to you."

"Now?" Cedric couldn't keep the hint of irritability out of his voice.

"Yes." Ouma only spoke Afrikaans. But he understood Afrikaans. It was useful. It enabled him to listen to his mother and Ouma skinnering. Sometimes they talked about him and Neil.

"I want you to promise me that you'll be gentle in the world."

What? He didn't see this coming.

"Will you promise me?" Ouma persisted.

Cedric didn't turn around. He studied the wall but his attention was directed backwards, to his Ouma. What sort of a thing was that to ask from him? Just when he was starting to think she was fine. He was a man, wasn't he? And sometimes a man needed to assert himself.

"Er, uhm."

His Ouma walked out.

ON A GOOD DAY

Jim tiptoed into the church. Late, as always, he was hoping to reach his seat in the fifth row without them noticing him. Flanked by his wife Emma, wet with perspiration from the rush, and his two children, Henry and Jessica, Jim bowed his head and shoulders, trying to look inconspicuous in the narrow aisle of the church, which was bursting with the Good Friday crowd.

His older brother, Dan, a lay minister, was at the altar. He was wearing a pious expression, hands in front of his chest, long fingers pointed at the sky. Bulbous eyes bulged from his head. He sang the loudest. His voice bludgeoned those of the choir and the congregation, curling round, strangling them in criticism of their reedy sound.

Dan's wife's scowl was the loudest.

Jim had to run this race every Sunday. He tried to reach his pew without attracting hostile stares from Dan and his wife, Clothilde, who had not spoken to them for the past seven years. But he was hopeful that today the full church would dilute their presence and he could enjoy the three-hour-long service.

On reaching his pew he shuffled in sideways. Emma followed, then the children. They were safe.

He had forgotten what the argument was about, but it had evolved into this awkwardness in church and whenever he met them at a relative's house or in the supermarket. It filled him with anxiety. He would greet and they would reply with a mean stare, causing giggles from onlookers who knew that they were related.

Dan had kicked Jim's shins regularly while they were growing up. That is, until their teens when, two years apart, Jim's growth spurt had resulted in him becoming bigger and taller. Dan never forgave him for that and for getting ten out of ten in all the spelling tests.

Jim opened his hymn book. They were already at the last verse. He tried to fit his baritone to the choir but his brother's overbearing voice made it difficult to follow, so he gave up, just looking at the words instead. Why sing so loud, he thought, glancing at Dan's tears, his habitual Good Friday grief. He cried at hospitals, funerals, weddings.

On the altar floor in front of Dan lay a wooden cross, two hammers and seven-centimetre nails.

The hymn came to an end and they sat down. Emma poked him in the ribs, pointed with her thumb. Diagonally across from them, his sister-in-law whipped her head around and gave them the full treatment. First she looked at him and Emma in disdain and then her glance shifted to their children. Her six children joined in, competing to outstare each other.

Little Henry, six years old, put his hand up to the side of his face as a blinker, to protect himself from the stares.

Jim noticed Henry's futile gesture; he saw Jessica curling her thin shoulders, trying to shrink into invisibility. The familiar anger rose in his heart. He got up, put Henry in his seat and shuffled past Emma and Jessica to sit at the end, leaning forward to use his body as a shield.

The starers did not flinch. He felt their eyes hammering his profile. They were frozen in hatred, in a parody of something he had seen on television.

Since his retrenchment he watched *My Little Pony* with his children, a show of multicoloured ponies with doll-hair manes. In one episode the ponies meet a cockatrice, a mythical creature with the head of a chicken and the body of a snake. The cockatrice's stare turns two of them into stone. One of the ponies then stares down the cockatrice with her own intimidating stare, becoming a stare master.

He wanted to glare at Clothilde. But in church?

Soon the ritual came of knocking nails into the cross to symbolise the crucifixion. People formed a long line stretching from the altar to the back of the church. More kept joining the throng. Tap-tap, the tinny sound of nails being driven into the cross was the only sound breaking the reverent silence.

As Jim neared the cross, he was filled with religious passion. He was going to leave all his sins, especially his anger, one of the seven deadly sins, on the cross. He knelt down, picked up the hammer and a nail. He was going to drive the nail in with one blow. He lifted the hammer up high... and the head flew off.

He stayed kneeling, unsure what to do. Someone handed him the spare. He looked up into his brother's cold eyes. Gripping the hammer with both hands, he lifted it up high and embedded the nail so deep there was only a shiny round orb visible above the rough wood. Around his nail, all the others stood up half in, resembling spines on a hedgehog.

Blindly, Jim stumbled to his seat. He could feel his brother's amphibian eyes boring into his back. He had had enough. Dan had made his life unbearable. And last year, even though they were not speaking, he had borrowed a chunk of Jim's severance pay. He had cried bitterly, saying one of his daughters needed an operation. Jim, with his soft heart, had given the money, which Dan had not returned.

He was going to pummel that crybaby right here in church. He spun round, into Emma's arms. She had anticipated the move. He allowed himself to be led to their bench. The anger boiled out of him. He needed to hit, to kick something. But he bowed his head and started breathing in deeply.

He looked up; the cockatrices were still staring, trying to turn him into stone. He wanted to get away, before he forgot himself.

The choir had started another hymn. As usual, his brother was running away with it. However, at the start of the third line something had happened to his voice. Years of abuse had worn through the vocal chords and his shouting tenor had disappeared.

Bereft of their accompaniment, the choir faltered. Clearly it came, another croaking sound, singing, "Jesus loves me! This I know, For the Bible tells me so."

RUNNING A STOP STREET

He had forgotten her birthday no he didn't yes he did and after she had made such a fuss of his bought him a watch and he gave her nothing didn't even remember What should she do Options Stand in front of the mirror and sing Happy Birthday to me no that won't do Take back the watch he won't even know he leaves it lying around it could just get lost no that would be wrong Talk about the people who had remembered say something like you know this guy at work he gave me such a kiss for my birthday full on the mouth that would show him no I don't want him to worry about me at work and insist that I stay home to look after the children I'm running out of ideas what about if I bought myself a present and open it in front of him or send flowers to myself saying it's from a secret admirer Now you're cooking more of the brilliant ideas Arrange a surprise party for my fortieth year and then when everyone jumps out and shouts surprise I won't be the only one surprised Forgive and move on no not after fifteen years you teach people how to treat you and if I do that what will I be doing but saying it's alright to forget my birthday the day I was born and came into this world so that he could find me and marry me I can't think of anything else I'm so hurt Does it mean he doesn't love me anymore I can't think like that a sure way to think myself into a depression He is the father of my six children the love of my life we have built a good life together oh damn this is so painful What should I do what talk to Maggie she always cheers me up Hi Maggie how are you he forgot my birthday Stop what are you saying you're not making any sense oh it's like running a stop street you know is there but you still go across without stopping Who would do that a stop sign is there for a reason to prevent chaos an accident it holds things together otherwise you have those slip-ways that look like a comma and the colons don't get me started on those colons robots littered across the landscape dot dot one on each side or those dashes a cul-de-sac going nowhere Oh sorry I apologise I got sidetracked not necessary to get so pedantic I know about the street Is that what he's doing he knows it's my birthday yes and he chose to ignore it oh it's like running a stop street you know is there but you still do it for your own reasons like punishment for something you did or didn't do or revenge or to prove that you don't have to obey the rules of communication What? &\ .,?-":;'/(-)!!

WINNING AND LOSING

"Winifred was their youngest child," Oom Baba said. He was the tall, angular man with wavy hair combed from a side parting and held in place with water and a fingertip of Vaseline.

"She was also the friendliest." He paused. "But she came from a strange family, believe me. Not one of the Oliphant children had teeth that grew into a straight line. There were rumours that their mother used to cut their gums with a razor to help them while they were teething. I heard it from my own wife who heard it from her mother who heard it from her best friend.

"The eldest boy had teeth growing all over the place in all directions. The second one's teeth were slightly better, and in the third boy's mouth only the eye teeth were about two spaces behind the others. The last child, Winifred, had almost perfect teeth. They grew in a straight line and only curved back slightly on both sides like a bird's wing." Oom Baba indicated how with his hands.

"Personally, I think there may be some truth in the story about their teeth. I mean, how do you explain that their teeth slowly got better, from the eldest to the youngest? In my opinion, it lends truth to the saying that practice makes perfect.

"Anyway, Winnie – everybody called her Winnie – was clever. You know, came first in her class, and won all the book prizes and so on.

She always had her nose in a book. They lived next to us and I don't know how many times her mother threatened to burn her books in the coal stove so that she could get on with her chores.

"She had her heart set on becoming someone who works in a library. You know, the one that chups your books and shows you where everything is. I saw one once when I took my grandson to the library." Oom Baba laughed, holding his stomach.

"Ja, Winnie said she wanted to spend her days surrounded by books. Other girls want to be surrounded by boyfriends, but she wanted to be surrounded by books.

"In her high school years she worked harder than ever because she had to get a bursary. Her parents were not rich, her father was an alcoholic. But towards the middle of standard seven, she started gaining weight and soon it became obvious that she was pregnant. We were all shocked because she had never showed any interest in boys. But that just goes to show you, stille waters, diepe grond, onder draai die duiwel rond. (Still water, deep ground, underneath the devil abounds.)

"The September exam was just around the corner and she worked like a madman for that exam. It was as if she wanted to pour all her dreams and the energy of future exams into that one exam." Oom Baba paused, sighed. "She scored almost full marks. Her teacher cried when he said that she would've achieved distinctions in all her subjects in matric and been the best pupil in the Transvaal, if not the whole country.

"The father of her child was a square fellow with curly hair. He had failed twice and was still in standard eight. Winnie's father said that no daughter of his would shame him by raising a child without a father, so instead of writing her final exam she got married at the end of that year.

"Years later, I heard that she was running a shebeen. It broke my heart. I went to visit, to see with my own eyes. She opened the door, two babies hanging onto her skirt. She had dark circles under her eyes."

Oom Baba shook his head, sad now. "Funny how children will have opportunities to better themselves, and still leave school to follow in the footsteps of their parents… Isn't it a funny thing, Ambrose?" He turned to look at his companion but Ambrose was fast asleep, leaning back in his chair with his mouth wide open.

CARE PLAN

The key component in looking after Derek was to provide holistic, individually focussed care.

Assessment
In a systematic way, Cathy collected and analysed data in order to make an assessment to establish his needs. Using verbal and non-verbal communication, focussed questions, sensitivity, warmth and empathy, she listened, clarifying to make sure she understood, and reflected on what he shared; adhering to guidelines for a good assessment.

Physiological
On examination, he had normal vital signs (temperature, pulse and blood pressure), was tall, big-boned and appeared healthy except for the occasional tic in his left eye. He had white teeth, a good posture.

Psychological
Of pleasant manner, he wasn't short-tempered. When tested he didn't display any signs of anxiety or irrational fears, although the tic appeared when he was stressed.

Socio-cultural
They shared the same background and had good nights.

Spiritual
He didn't go to church. She was a devout Catholic.

Economic
He had a good job as a marketing executive and paid for dinner. He currently owned a car, as well as a budgie.

Lifestyle
He went to the gym, liked to play tennis, eat out, and go dancing. He didn't flirt with other women when he was with her.

Diagnosis
He was eminently suitable. He could get out of bed, had a good appetite, and didn't present with withdrawal symptoms. He didn't have other problems, such as conflict with her family or the potential to cause complications.

Planning
Based on the assessment and diagnosis, Cathy set objective, measurable and achievable short- and long-term goals; moving from her city to his, maintaining good nutrition by providing meals three times a day, and resolving to settle conflict through exchange of viewpoints.

Assessment data, diagnosis, and goals were written down in her memory so that others caring for him would have access to it.

Implementation
His care would be implemented at least twice in 24 hours, according to the plan. Continuity of care during their time together and in preparation for a long marriage was therefore assured. It would be documented in the relationship's record.

A professional care giver, she was selfless, nurturing, and prioritised others, abandoning self-care, managing the effects of an abused childhood through medication.

Evaluation

The status and efficacy of her evidence-based care plan would be continuously assessed and modified as needed.

MOVING IN

Oom Bollie couldn't remember where he was. Lifting his head, he saw the familiar red-brown earth of his wife's grave underneath him. He got up stiffly, flexing his limbs to get the circulation going, to relieve the numbness in his fingers and toes.

He had too much to drink last night.

He believed that a man went through three different stages when drinking. During the first stage, which lasted roughly up to the third glass, he was overcome by an incredible feeling of goodwill and love for mankind.

This feeling couldn't be rivalled by anything else in the world. It was mainly for this reason that he frequented the shebeens. He wasn't a heavy drinker.

Basically, he was a happy person, and it was only in the shebeen where he came into his own, strumming his guitar and singing all the ribald songs he loved to make up.

His favourite drinking song went like this: "More omie more tannie waar is Sannie dan. Sannie het gaan water skep daar onder in die vlei. Sannie se rokkie het 'n skeurtjie in, die jongspan loer daardeur. Die jongspan vra om haar te vry. Oe la la la-la la." The chorus was "Daar was 'n dooie hoenerhaan. Daar was 'n dooie kallekoen." The other one involved a donkey.

The second stage of drinking, which lasted from about the fourth to the sixth glass, could go two ways. Some men discovered how strong they were and wanted to fight. These were friends to avoid. He preferred the ones who started crying at this stage, because that was generally what he did.

The third stage, which he called being reckless, was when your common sense left you and you made a fool of yourself. And what was worse, you couldn't remember what you did the next day. Ja-nee (yes-no), he had too much to drink last night. It was between these last two stages that he came to cry on his wife's grave, when the loneliness overcame him.

Standing in front of the grave, he felt a momentary contraction of his heart. Five years. And not even a child to cushion his life. He picked up a small stone and placed it on the grave in greeting. After saying a short prayer he set about pulling out the weeds.

On his way out he noticed a new tombstone. It was taller, bigger, than all the others. 'In loving memory of my husband William Snell' he read. He knew William; quiet, morose, with sores on his head that wouldn't heal. Two years ago he had landed under a bus that was supposed to take him to work.

He decided to call on William's widow. It was the ideal time. She was probably on her way to church right now, but that gave him enough time to shave, polish his shoes, and even go for a haircut. His best friend, Alfie, was good with clippers.

Alfie was in his socks, reading the Sunday Times Extra, a special edition of Coloured and Indian news; another edition with Bantu news was sold in black townships. The smell of roast potatoes filled the small lounge.

"Bollie, howzit, my brother? Come in. The wife is busy in the kitchen."

"Ou, Alf. I was wondering if you could give me a haircut."

"Bollie, my man, you know I would do it for you, but the wife… It's Sunday, man. She'll say the hair will fly into the food."

"We could do it outside."

"The preacher will see us. He lives next door and he'll tell my wife. It's not that I'm afraid of her, but a man has to keep things sweet. You understand." He looked at Bollie, suspicious. "Why do you want a haircut now? Your haircut is only due in two weeks?"

"No reason. Cheers. See you." Oom Bollie hurried out.

Later he stood in front of the small mirror stuck on the wall of his room in his sister's house. He brushed his red hair carefully. Fifty-nine, and not a single grey hair. Peering into the mirror, he brushed his cheeks with the palm of his hand as if flicking dust from a coat. It was an unconscious habit held over from childhood, when the other boys had teased him about his freckles. Boere, they had called him.

In another habit acquired from his short stint in the police force, he buffed his shoes until they shone. From his bedside table he took the aftershave lotion given to him as a present and which he saved for special occasions. He poured a little on his hand and slapped it on his cheeks in the manner of the advertisements on television.

He considered taking his guitar. Women liked that sort of thing. But he decided against it. Another time. First, he had to get his foot in the door. He had not been so tense since his wedding day.

"Good afternoon, sister," Oom Bollie said. He was standing on the doorstep twirling his hat.

"Why, hello, Bollie." Mary Snell put a hand on her ample bosom. "How are you? My, I haven't seen you for a while. Since William's funeral. How is your sister? And the little ones?" She spoke rapidly, short of breath. "Please come in." She moved to allow him to pass.

He entered, stood in the middle of the dining-cum-sitting room, twirling his hat.

"Please sit down," she said, waving her hand in the direction of the sofa.

He sat down on the edge, hung his hat on his knee. It fell down. He picked it up and clasped it in front of him. During the silence that followed, his eyes travelled around the room. He noticed the new hi-fi set standing in the corner.

"How do you like it?" Mary had followed his gaze. "William always promised he would buy me a hi-fi one day. But now…" she faltered, sighing deeply.

Oom Bollie nodded. "William was a good man."

"Yes, and so generous," Mary said. "That is why I think he would not have minded me buying the hi-fi."

"William was a kind and generous man," Oom Bollie agreed.

"Do you know what I miss most?" Mary's eyes became moist. "His kindness and his sense of humour."

"Ja-nee," Oom Bollie said. It didn't matter that William was a man who spent more time at home than he did working, and that his sense of humour consisted of practical jokes like leaning a slop bucket against someone's door on New Year's Eve.

"How are you coping?" Oom Bollie fixed his dark-brown eyes on Mary's face. She was ten years younger, still pretty. She had gained weight since he last saw her. He smiled, approving. A man liked biltong in meat but not in women. Her nails were long and red; her glossy black hair cut in a new style.

"Holding up, holding up, Bollie." She blushed slightly. "You?"

"I'm fine." After a long silence, he got up, cleared his throat. "I just came to see how you were."

"Would you like a cup of coffee?"

"Yes, please." Oom Bollie sat down again.

She disappeared into the kitchen. He leaned back and listened to the small sounds she made while making the coffee. She reappeared with a tray. He jumped up, uncertain whether to take it or not. She walked past him and placed the tray on the coffee table, poured his coffee. She held out a plate of koeksisters. He took one eagerly. They were fat, brown with spice, dunked in light syrup, and rolled in coconut.

He saw a knobkierie, a walking stick, with an ornate handle next to the couch. In the shape of a T with one arm shorter, it had an intricate carving of a bird. "What a lovely stick." He touched it reverently. As a cabinet maker, he appreciated the beauty of wood.

"It belonged to my father." Mary's eyes were teary again.

"How is Michael?" Oom Bollie said, to head her off; women's tears made him weak in the knees. Michael was her neighbour.

"He bought a second-hand car."

"Really? A new car, hey."

They discussed the exorbitant price, make, colour and new gadgets of Michael's car.

Oom Bollie got up to go. "Please let me know if there's anything, anything at all, that I can do to help." He walked towards the door. With his hand on the doorknob, he looked back. She was standing uncertainly in front of her chair. Realising that he was wet with perspiration, he yanked open the door. "Bye."

Mary came forward. "Bye. Give my regards to your sister."

On Monday morning, Oom Bollie whistled cheerfully while getting ready for work. In the week that followed, Mary's face was never far from his consciousness. It framed his days, his existence, like the gilt edge of a portrait.

Sunday afternoon after lunch, Mary sent a message with her youngest son. Oom Bollie was to come immediately. He rushed through his toilette before walking over to her house.

"Oh, Bollie, I'm so glad you came," she said, on opening the door. "I'm so upset. Billy Solomon was here. You know how he is, going around on his bicycle visiting all the women whose husbands have died. The way he looked at me, Bollie! And my husband not even cold in his grave. I gave him a piece of my mind. Imagine. I wonder who he thinks he is, and him being as dark as night like those Madras Indians."

Oom Bollie tried his best to soothe Mary. The cheek of Billy Solomon. Privately he felt uneasy though, like a man caught sipping someone else's beer. He could not go near her house for two months.

Then he heard that Billy Solomon was seen leaving Mary's house. He rushed over on the same day. Mary greeted him with a coy laugh. She seemed changed somehow, sort of animated by an inner glow of mystery. Oom Bollie stood in the doorway, twirling his hat. He wanted to ask if it was true that Billy had been there, but couldn't.

"Come in," Mary said, skipping to the lounge.

He seated himself on a chair near the door.

"Billy was here," Mary said after a while. "You know, Bollie, he is not so bad. He's quite a nice man."

"Hmm," Oom Bollie grunted. It was now or never, he thought. He cleared his throat. "Things have changed in the world. People are so cold nowadays. They take advantage of your weakness. They are not interested in helping a friend. But you need never worry about me, Mary, you can call on me any time, whenever you like." He paused. "I also have the greatest respect for you." Oom Bollie had been looking at the floor. He stopped when he felt Mary's soft body leaning against him.

A week later he met Billy at the bus stop. "Congratulations," Billy said. He winked conspiratorially. "Well done, brother. I heard you moved in with Mary Snell. Lekker vat en sit. She is a strange one, though. Last week she called me over to fix her son's bicycle. Naturally, being a red-blooded man, I thought it was just an excuse to get me there. But she slapped my hand when I put it on her knee. You must watch out. They say she is a tiger."

True to the heritage of his red hair, Oom Bollie's temper flared and his fist ended Billy's conversation.

Six months later, Mary declared the shebeen a bad place, only for ungodly people. Oom Bollie stopped playing his guitar; she didn't like the words he put to his songs.

"They are not fit for decent people and children," she said.

He didn't go back to the shebeen, but one morning, missing his previous life, he called the shebeen queen and asked her to send over a six-pack to share with friends.

Screaming at him in a new shrill voice he hadn't heard before, Mary broke the beers on her rock garden. When she came back, she grabbed the knobkierie.

GETTING ALONG

"What a lovely sunset," he said. He could sense her hostility. She had said nothing on the drive from their home in Sandton to the isolated beach cottage they had hired for the week in Durban.

"Would you like a drink?" She came upright in her deckchair.

A peace offering; he was happy. "A Coke, please," he said. They were here on the advice of their marriage counsellor but already he was feeling the strain.

By the time she returned, he had changed his mind. "Thanks. I'll drink it later." What if she tried to poison him? She was capable of killing him, but not if he got to her first.

"Suit yourself."

The sun was getting weaker. The long shadow of a branch from the tree above them had displaced its warmth.

"So, what should we do tomorrow?" He was exhausted, trying to get along with this woman.

"I'm not going anywhere with you."

His temples throbbed. His mind hooked on the word 'strangle'. He jumped up and went inside.

LEAVING HER

Ed waited for Marina outside the lecture room where she was teaching biology. He was using her car, and had dropped her off that morning. In vain he opened the driver's door to snag a breeze. Heat misted up his spectacles.

Irritably he removed them and wiped a callused hand across his face. He hated waiting, and wished that he had an appointment. But his plumbing business wasn't doing as well as he had hoped. Financed by Marina's father, it was supposed to bring him independence. Yet the closed corporation struggled along, necessitating loans from her uncle to pay his workers, which reminded him that he had to ask her to ask her father...

"Fok," he said under his breath. To escape the suffocating heat in the car, he slouched into the lecture room, pulling up his trousers. They sat on his stomach for a second, then sagged down, hanging around his hips, creasing on top of his shoes; the seams at the back of the trouser-legs dirty and worn from being stepped on.

He hoped not to meet any of her colleagues. They looked down their noses at him.

When he reached the door, he peeped in. The pimply youngsters in her class were as bored as he was after listening to her for more than a minute. She had an annoying voice, high-pitched and wheedling. Enough. He went to her small office at the side of the building.

Her handbag was there. He opened it, looking for money. She never missed a few twenties, the dumb witch. What was that smell? Something was wrapped in a plastic packet. *She couldn't keep secrets from him, they were married.* Opening it, his nostrils flared at the assault on his olfactory senses. A dead rat, neatly wrapped.

Holding it as far from him as the length of his arm, he stomped out of the office.

෧

A rat had come in through the fireplace of their home the previous night. It had skirted the dining room wall, hiding under the couches as it scurried along.

Marina had only seen it when it had to cross the entrance hall floor to get to the kitchen. The rat had stopped at the door jamb.

Thoughts about the pellets, the dreadful black pellets in the oats, the flour and the sugar, had flooded her mind. "Go away," she had shouted.

She had called Ed but he had not heard her. He was her protector. Once, she had drawn a picture of herself in profile, pregnant, looking up into the rays of an all-enveloping sun. Ed was that sun.

෧

Marina's court shoes tapped on the tiles to her office. Dressed in a powder-blue suit with a long skirt, her hair was scraped back in a severe bun. The stifling heat had squeezed sweat droplets through her make-up.

She was looking for her face powder in her handbag when she discovered that the rat was gone. Who could've taken it? Her husband… Sometimes he looked for a tissue because he thought it effeminate to carry tissues in his own pocket.

She nodded fondly; theirs was a marriage smiled upon by angels. He was a wonderful man, although everyone always asked what she was doing with an illiterate boy.

But she had to keep him out of her bag.

In the humid silence on the way home (he was driving), she glanced at him from under her lashes. Would he ask about the rat? She doubted it.

They never spoke about things that could seep under the gossamer fabric of smiles and jokes that punctuated their relationship. But if he asked, she'd feign innocence, say that her class probably put it there.

❧

He came to her in the kitchen where she was making his favourite supper, sausages and rice. She looked up with a welcoming smile.

"I want a divorce," he said, before turning away.

"What?" She licked her lips. "But, we can't…. The baby…"

He had gone from the room.

She started crying, thinking that she should've bought that lounge suite and stored it at her sister's house. And, of course, the rat poison.

The next morning she made breakfast. He ate his cornflakes with a sprinkling of bran – brown pellets that almost looked like rat droppings. She made coffee, black as usual, and carried the tray to the bedroom. He was sitting on the side of the bed, his head in his hands.

"I really want a divorce," he said.

To give herself a chance to think, she dropped the tray. She knelt on the floor, scraping cornflakes and bran back onto the plate.

"I can't carry on like this. I need a new business partner."

"Do you have someone in mind?"

"Yes. In fact, we just have to draw up the papers."

She sat back on her haunches. The bran pellets on the floor, soaked with coffee, had darkened in colour.

"Who is he… she… your business partner?"

"Someone you don't know." He had threatened to leave before.

"But... I love you."

"I know," he said airily, scratching his armpit. "Now, go get me my breakfast."

"Of course, honey."

On the way out she thought about her shopping list. She cursed the oppressive heat. It ought to rain.

OPPOSITES ATTRACT

hearts.

Beauty is a strange thing. It is not the mere aesthetic appearance of things, as many people have come to believe. It is not a summer's day, or a flower, or the filmy fluttering of a thin skirt about the ankles of a person who might or might not be a descendant of Venus. Beauty is not in the eye of the beholder. There can be no description of true beauty; the minute you turn to examine it, it evaporates and loses its colour. It can never be seen. It is invisible. It is not sudden, and its entrance into your mind can neither be felt nor remembered. When it leaves, you will not notice until it is completely gone. And even then, it is only because you remember a feeling of serenity that you seem to have misplaced. When you feel beauty, it vibrates with a melodic humming within your centre. It fills you with the need to sigh and look up and find more beauty around you; in the trees, in the faces of your loved ones, as a whisper on the breeze. It fills you completely, and you want for nothing. You realise true peace for that fleeting instant. You hold no grudges, and though you may cry tears, the emotion producing them can no more be explained than the flooding of your heart with that quiet joy that can only come from heaven. And while the beauty lasts, you understand that it is not in the eye of the beholder, but in their spirit.

Hatred is a strange thing. It is not a winter's day, or an ugly weed, or the threatening flight of a crow above the head of a partner who might or might not be a descendant of Erida. There can be no description of true hatred; the minute you turn to examine it, it evaporates and loses its colour. It is not sudden, and its entrance into your mind can neither be felt nor remembered. When it leaves, you will not notice until it is completely gone. And even then, it is only because you suddenly remember a darkness that you seem to have misplaced. When you feel hatred, it vibrates with discordance in your soul. It fills you with the need to destroy, to search and find more hate around you; in the trees, in the faces of your loved ones, as a whisper on the breeze. You hold grudges, and though you may cry tears, the emotion producing them can no more be explained than the flooding of your heart with hate and loathing that can only come from the alienation of beauty. And while the hatred lasts, you will understand. It is not in the eye of the beholder, but in their

IN THE BIBLE

He pined for the beauty of the recent past; law and order, prosperity and everyone knowing their place. It was a life of barbecues, sunny skies and dancing in your own swimming pool. A deep sigh rucked up from the bottom of his barrel chest. He leaned back in the chair, running both hands through his thick, brown hair. Black half-moons of grime lay under his fingernails.

He didn't belong. A duck without water, that's how he saw himself in the new strange land that had sprung up around him, alien, a nightmare. Here he had been declared an oppressor, and was regarded with suspicion. Here he had to field demands for explanations about the past.

How could he answer when he didn't know what they were talking about? Everyone wanted to be surrounded by their own. The ducks belonged with the ducks, the rhinos with the rhinos and the bees with the bees; a place for everything and everyone.

He sighed again, looking at his nails. He nibbled at one, tasting the dirt. In the past, he had never met other races except as maids and gardeners, but now they were everywhere; in schools, restaurants, the cinema, in the parks. It was stressful. And because they had been elevated to go where he went, they were not so respectful anymore. Others were downright cheeky.

Whack.

He had developed the uncontrollable urge to punch an object. This manifested in him lifting his right hand and bringing it down hard to strike the air every few minutes, a habit that had become debilitating.

People turned to stare when he walked in the streets, and his wife, Liefie, and their two sons had nagged him to see a psychiatrist. He swore. There was too much dependence on that rubbish nowadays. Nobody could just let you be.

His solution was to withdraw into a bunker, waiting for better days. A portable television set stood on a low table in front of him; next to it a Bible. There was something wrong with the television's aerial but he didn't have the energy to have it fixed.

Sometimes he spoke to his father, long dead. He would've liked to speak to Liefie, but she had left him, taking most of the furniture. Because he had been rude to his son's wife.

"I'm not a racist. Everybody's so damn sensitive. It's better to sit here, because out there everybody's talking about racism, anti-racism, non-racialism and heaven knows what else.

"It makes me uncomfortable when they talk like that. It's like they're saying I'm a bad person, and I'm not. So I'm sitting here and I'm hurting nobody. I read my Bible.

"I have principles. I used to go to the Dutch Reformed Church on Sunday. I'm an individual. How can I be held responsible for what other people have done? I didn't do anything. Forgive and move on."

The transformation had not been good for him. He missed the gentility of a past where things were done in a certain way. But that was no longer accepted. And he liked routine.

"I tried, Pa, heaven knows I tried. I registered my domestic worker and paid her more than the recommended wage. I put her son through school. But it was never enough."

Whack.

"It's like there's no place for me out there. So I'm in here. But I have everything I need. When I'm hungry, I just go into my bedroom and open a tin. I have stacks of them against the walls, piled up to the ceiling. Bully beef, baked beans, spaghetti, peas, lentils, pilchards, sardines. I drink water from the borehole. It's not as clear as it used to be but what can you expect? There's no one to dig; the gardener also left."

He pulled on his long beard. "And there are too many foreigners."

He deplored the influx of new businesses. Chinese malls selling cheap clothes, Pakistani cell phone repair shops, Nigerian tailors. The garment industry was under threat. His clothes store, which he had run for fourteen years, had gone under. Whack.

These immigrants contributed to the strange land becoming stranger. Being a businessman, he knew that there was money to be made at the rise and fall of civilisations, but there were too many foreigners and ragged people coming into the cities.

"They say I was privileged, Pa. Where was I privileged? I worked hard for everything I have – my house, my swimming pool, the plot in Honeydew.

"And I always did the right thing. As boss and father, I ruled with an iron hand and conducted religious services in my home at night. God had given us this land, right? It says so in the Bible. But the church has apologised. For what? I'm confused. I'm glad you're not here to see what has happened."

He walked to get a tin of pilchards, opened it, and ate from the tin standing up, fishing out the bony parts with his fingers. He dipped a slice of old bread, folded in half, into the sauce, chewing thoughtfully.

"How could apartheid have harmed people when it was separate but equal? Each person in his own place, developing at his own pace.

"And we didn't do it alone. Remember, the English came before us. Why not just get over it?"

In the shelter of his wealth he couldn't see a link between the policies of dispossession and him having access to the capital to start his clothing franchise.

He walked back to his chair. Leaning forward, he took the Bible. The biceps muscle of his right arm was bigger than the left.

His shoulder ached because of the constant movement. He paged through. He found solace in his Bible. Inside it was another book.

"I have a companion to my Bible, Pa. It explains everything. For example, where do black and Coloured people come from?" He laughed. "It shows me where to look for an answer. Hosea 7:8 and Exodus 13:11. You would've liked this little book. It has all the answers at your fingertips.

"My favourite book is Genesis, especially the story about the sons of Noah: Shem, Ham and Japheth. I also like Psalm 105:44, 'And He gave them the lands of the nations, and they inherited labour of the people, they took possession'.

"Now we have the church apologising, saying that they were wrong. How could they be wrong? I grew up with these verses, I believe in them and I'm too old to change."

He had lived according to the teachings of the Bible, especially the Old Testament. Abraham's God, his father's God. He found it impossible to accept that it could be interpreted in an erroneous way. It was unthinkable that anyone could've messed with religion. It was sacred.

"I know we have a brutal past, but… We had to survive. I am what I am, and Liefie shouldn't have expected me to change. It was the shock, you see. My son bringing home a…"

He believed that his people should not combine with others. He could quote various verses in support of this. Joshua 23:7, 'That you with these nations, with you left together, do not mix'; Ezra 9:12, 'And now, not your daughters to their sons, or take their daughters for your sons'; Deuteronomy 7:3, 'You shall not intermarry with them'; Verse 4, 'For then shall be kindled against you the wrath of the Lord, and He will destroy you'.

In spite of this, his son had married a black girl and she had produced his first grandson. What did you teach such a child, he pondered, scraping his spoon around the bottom of the tin and licking it. With his own children, he had re-enacted the Anglo-Boer war. He would hide and the little Boer generals would seek him out with toy guns.

But this new child. Would he hate with his heart, a passion that would burn itself out, or with his mind, cold, clinical, that could last for generations? Would he be lazy, have low morals and be inherently violent? Would he learn how to dominate others?

He threw the tin onto a growing pile, remembered he had to take out the garbage. When did they collect again? Liefie would've known. He hacked up phlegm, spat it into his handkerchief.

Because the land had changed so much, and he was struggling, he believed that the end of the world was upon him. His views coincided, found an echo, in the fundamentalist churches, and he had been able to access a new clutch of Bible verses, and another companion booklet about the theology of the End Times.

That book, however, had been lost. With the turmoil of Liefie packing up and leaving, and his youngest son moving out, he didn't know where to search for it. Whack.

The K-word, a derogatory term; K, k, k, that was what he had called Johan's wife. In the American South after the war, the Ku Klux Klan had risen from the gentlemen of the plantation class, to deal with the influx of Yankee carpetbaggers and cheeky Negroes. He had read that somewhere. He had also heard that there was such an organisation online. Created in 1995 for white supremacists like him, like Breivik, it was founded by a previous Grand Wizard of the KKK.

Normally he would've supported it, but then there was the child, a four-year-old with large black eyes, innocent eyes. He suspected that he would kill anyone who harmed a hair on his head, or would he? Whack.

SHADOW KIDS

3 June 1989
Dear Diary,

Mummy-One chose a good family for me. Nobody knows because it's a secret. My new father is a principal. I've no other father because I don't know who my real father is.

She gives money every month. I don't see it because it's expensive to raise children. That's what my other mummy, Mummy-Two says.

But how I wish I could go and live with my own mother.

Mummy-One says the reason is in Deuteronomy 23, Verse 2: *Geen baster mag in die vergadering van die Here kom nie.* She says they deleted it from the new Bible, but it still stands. That's why I can't live with her. I won't be able to go to church.

5 June 1989
Dear Diary,

No more wild hair and ashy legs! I straightened my hair and bought coco butter for my legs.

I was so excited. For once my coarse hair lies flat instead of standing up like grass. My new hair is almost like my mother's. She has blonde hair that is soft. When I was smaller I used to touch it all the time. But she says I'm too big for that now.

I tied my hair in a big bow to show off to Mummy-One. She touched it and said it's nice, it feels like mielie hair.

7 June 1989
Dear Diary,

~~A girl in my school called Edna also has a white mother. Shh. I'm not supposed to tell. It's a big secret. My parents have sworn never to tell. My friends don't know. I'm only telling you, dear diary, because you are my best friend.~~

Edna was given to the priest, Father Evans. She says they are good to her, but she misses her real mother, even though she has never lived with her. Her mother doesn't want to see her. She just sends money every month.

Edna is five years older than me. Sixteen. She has light skin. She says if she was lighter she could've gone to live with her mother. The problem was her ears. The person who looked said there was dark skin around the edges. That counted against her. She hates her ears.

She wants to join the struggle to fight for the right to see her mother. She says we are the shadow kids. We were dumped by our parents who broke the laws of the land long after they were made and gave their children to leaders in our community who adopted us.

We are in hiding. Nobody knows we exist. If people find out we'll be in trouble. Shh.

My mother is Afrikaans but hers is Italian. She knows who her father is. He was from Malawi. I wonder who my father is.

There's another boy. I don't know him well. He was the only dark one in his family. When people came to visit he had to hide. It became bad. They had to give him away.

When he was older he went to visit his family. 'What do you want?' they asked. 'We've written you off already.' Now he is so angry. I'm afraid of him. He stabs everybody.

Like
Straight hair, white skin
Don't like

Coarse hair, dark skin

Mummy-One doesn't approve of me. I can see it in her eyes. She wipes my face hard as if she wants to scrub the dark away. Pulls at my hair as if she wishes she can change it. I'm such a disappointment.

I'm lucky to have a beautiful mother. If I could I would be as white as snow with blue-blue eyes. Sometimes I put a pillow on my head and swish it around, pretending I have straight hair.

15 June 1989
Dear Diary,

It's my birthday today. I have pips in my breasts. It hurts. I wish I could show Mummy-One.

I HATE white people because they keep us apart. That's what my mother says. That I can't stay with her because of them.

She has two other children, but they don't know about me. I've seen them from far. They must never know about me. About the shame I bring on them. I must carry it all by myself. I feel guilty.

20 June 1989
Dear Diary,

When Mummy-One is angry she says I'm Gam se kind. It hurts me because I don't understand. Gam is someone who caused a lot of trouble in the Bible because he saw his father naked. He was cursed to serve his brothers.

PS. If I got my dark skin from my father, how did Gam get to be my dad?

25 June 1989
Dear Diary,

I know I shouldn't say it, but I HATE it when she talks like that. It makes me afraid of her. She gets this funny look in her eyes.

She says Afrikaners are God's chosen people. The Israelites. It says so in the Bible. David and Solomon were white. Moses was white.

The chosen people are not allowed to mix with heathens. What does it mean? I don't want to lose my mother! I feel the fear choking me.

Am I a heathen? Even if I go to church on Sundays and sing in the choir? Because I think my father may be black. Shh. Why else would I have such a dark skin?

30 June 1989
Dear Diary,

I'm so sad. I've been crying for weeks now. I HATE watermelon. It made me mess up my friendship with Mummy-One. I call her that because she is my birth mother. My adopted mother I call Mummy-Two. But that's my secret; they don't know I call them that.

I took the bus to my mother's place like I do every three months. We went on a picnic out in the veld. She doesn't like people to see us together. She says they will talk.

She brought chicken wings and the watermelon was for dessert. I love watermelon +++. There was a whole watermelon just for the two of us. At Mummy-Two's place we only have two slices each because there are nine children; and the adults get the crowns.

At the picnic I could eat as many slices and crowns as I wanted. I ate till my stomach was sore. Mummy-One was upset. She won't let me come again, I just know it. She asked what they were teaching me in that dusty, godforsaken place.

I'm such a greedy pig. A disgrace. I just know she won't let me visit her again. What will become of me? How will I survive without her? I'm not eating watermelon again. EVER. Cross my heart and hope to die. May the lightning strike me if I lie.

PS. Please God, let me visit her. I will be good. I will become a nun and serve you forever.

30 July 1989
I have not heard from Mummy-One. She used to phone me once a month. I miss her.

15 August 1989
I STILL have not heard from her. I'm worried. Maybe something happened to her. There is so much crime. Dear Lord, please look after my mother.

30 September 1989
I was worried, but now I'm afraid. Dare I think it? It's not fair to Mummy-One. She has always been good to me. But. Maybe. Maybe she's not coming back? Mummy-Two says she's a lovely woman and she adores me. But where is she????

3 April 1990
Mummy-Two says trust in the Lord. I am trusting in the Lord, but I'm losing hope. It's almost a year. Edna says she made a run for it, but I don't believe her. She's just jealous because I have my mother and she doesn't. So, pear. Pear-wear-wear-wear-wear. You don't have a mo-ther.

27 April 1994
FINALLY. South Africa is free and I can go and stay with my own mother. Yippee!

30 July 1996
Right. I can stay with Mummy-One. If she arrives. At this stage I have my doubts. I think. Maybe I will just stay where I am. Mummy-Two, Father, and all my noisy brothers and sisters who get on my <u>nerves</u> (underlined in three different colours). They love me.

LOVE AT FIRST BITE

The sun dipped behind the mountain, leaving vivid orange streaks among floating, dark, almost-black clouds as a souvenir of what they had just witnessed: the purple and yellow pyrotechnic display of an African sunset.

"That was stunning, wasn't it?" Lydia sighed.

"I arranged it all for you." Tyrone turned towards her in the deckchair and smiled lazily.

His topaz eyes flicked over her bikini. They'd just met at the beach and she hadn't had time to change. He was handsome, in brown shorts, a canvas bag slung over his shoulder.

Her heart stopped. Did she imagine it or was there admiration in those mysterious eyes? He was devastatingly attractive with his dark mane and even, white teeth. He stretched out his long legs in front of him.

"Wait till you see what I have planned for later."

"Dinner, I hope," she said. "I'm starving." Immediately she regretted talking about such a mundane thing as eating in the presence of love. Because that is what she felt for him, an instant attraction which could develop into an abiding, forever kind of love. There was such a thing as love at first sight, after all.

"Of course," he laughed. "I like a girl who can eat."

Was he teasing her? She wasn't sure; she was curvy.

"You're perfect," he said, as if reading her thoughts.

"Thanks."

"I have a surprise for you. It's in my bag." He went into her cottage. Presently he came out carrying a bottle of sparkling wine and two glasses.

"What's this?" she said breathlessly. Her dream was about to come true. He would stay the night and they would live happily ever after.

"Something to celebrate." He uncorked the bottle.

Her mind turned to fast forward and she saw nappies and talcum powder, pretty babies smiling with rosy cheeks out of calm photographs. Then it reversed; whoa, girl, take it easy, she reminded herself. He poured, handed her a glass. She sipped delicately.

"So, what is it you do for work again?" She had not really listened the first time he'd told her.

A dark-red flush coloured his cheeks. "I'm a painter."

"An artist, oh I love the arts," she said enthusiastically.

"No," his discomfort was palpable, "I paint houses. I can paint a four-room house in one day."

"Oh." Her eyes narrowed. She had been too hasty. But he had money for champagne... "Do you have your own company?"

"No, I work for someone else."

"I hope you don't mind, but I have to ask: where did you get the champagne?"

"I took it on credit."

Hell no. The last thing she needed was a man who couldn't pay his bills. The next thing you know, he will be asking her to put clothes on his ass. She had definitely been too hasty in inviting him into her holiday home, her little cottage near the sea. Which she had acquired in the divorce settlement. Where she came to get away from the stress of her busy life.

But he was so cute, lean body, muscular arms, and bubble butt. He'd better be good in bed. She tried to sneak a look at his thighs. He saw her looking; a little smile started near the corner of his mouth. She flushed crimson.

At that moment her ex-husband, Colin, walked in. He pulled a chair up, uninvited, to sit next to her. She inhaled sharply. Every dog is supposed to have his day, but this bulldog, who's supposed to have a weekend, just keeps escaping. He was a mining engineer and she had prayed many times that the earth would fall in and bury him.

"Well, if it isn't Mr Scrooge himself. What are you doing here? Are you following me?"

"Don't flatter yourself."

"You're not getting this place back. It's enough you have my dog." Her voice had changed. It was bathed in venom.

"I don't want it back. You can keep it." Colin flicked his wrist.

"How's Mitzy?" Vulnerability had crept into her voice.

"She's fine. Better than ever. There's nobody around to give her junk food."

"Humph."

Tyrone coughed. Colin turned to him. "Hi, bro," he said. "Are you here to clean the pool?"

"Excuse me?" Tyrone sat forward in his chair.

"Don't worry about him, he's nobody. As a matter of fact," she came erect, pulling herself to her full height of 156 cm, throwing dagger eyes at Colin. "We were just on our way out. Tyrone here is an artist."

"I'm a painter…" Tyrone extended his hand. Colin ignored it.

"An artist," Lydia repeated firmly.

"Interesting." Colin's eyes raked over Tyrone's long frame distastefully. "And what do you paint? I just hate what passes for art these days."

Before Tyrone could answer, Lydia came to sit on his lap. "He's a famous artist. But you wouldn't know because you're a caveman. You wouldn't know good art if it bit you on your hard hat."

Tyrone shifted uncomfortably. She planted her arms around his neck. "If you'll excuse us, we were just on our way to dinner."

Colin remained seated, yawned. "Where're you going?"

"To this new place that opened near the garage."

Tyrone put his mouth close to her ear and whispered, "I don't have money... for a... a restaurant. I used it all for the champagne. I was thinking... I could cook? I live nearby. Pap (porridge) and steak, maybe?"

Lydia giggled as if he had just made a lewd suggestion. To Colin: "As you can see, we're busy."

Colin leaned over, picked up a dog-eared Mills & Boon novel from her chair. "Are you still reading this junk?"

"Do you want me to throw him out?" Tyrone whispered.

"No." She planted a kiss on his mouth. He bit her lip, drawing blood.

"Aren't we passionate," she said, giggling again. "Bye, Colin. May the door hit you on your way out. And I'm coming for my dog. If I had a child, you would probably have kept that too, you spiteful pig."

"The dog is better off living with me," Colin said calmly, getting up to leave. "But you can come by anytime to visit."

When he was out the door, Tyrone leaned in for a passionate kiss but she pushed him away.

"Not so fast, tiger." She smiled. A drop of blood slid from her lip to her chin, from there onto her breast.

"Did you just use me to make your ex jealous?" Tyrone frowned.

"Of course not. I like you, a lot. Now, what did you say about pap and steak?"

"I could make it here."

"No. I don't want pap burning my Le Creuset pots."

"Your what?"

"Don't worry your pretty little head about it. Let's go."

Today, instead of fine dining she would mingle with the masses and have wild, animal sex.

"No," he said.

"What?" A man saying no to a quick tumble? What was he? A eunuch?

"I may not have money, but I have my pride. And I'm not stupid. I can see that you look down on me." He untangled his long frame. "Good evening."

"Hey, wait. I didn't mean it like that. I'm sorry if I hurt your feelings."

"You did," he said stubbornly.

"I'm really sorry. I wasn't thinking. My ex upsets me so much. Will you forgive me? Please?"

"Okay." He sat down again. "My name is Tyrone Wilkins and I'm a painter… of houses."

"My name is Lydia Simons and I own a communications company."

"Phew. Are you rich?"

"Not as much as I'd like to be. I want to be a millionaire before I'm fifty."

He laughed, a deep rumble that came out of his belly. It tickled her iliac bones. "And I'm poor, but not as poor as I could be. I'm a poet, a killer poet."

She was delighted. "So you _are_ in the arts."

"You could say that."

"Cool. Big ups. Super, smashing, and all that."

"Why didn't you want me to throw out your ex?"

"Colin? Because he's not worth it. Now, can you please stop talking about that horrid man and take me to your place. I would love to hear some of your poetry."

STAGE FRIGHT

Anna was the proverbial fish out of water. People were different in the city, more sophisticated. Not like the simple folks at home who greeted all and sundry; as she did once, addressing a young girl in the lift, only to be met with silence.

It had unnerved her, caused her to enter the lift with downcast eyes like everyone else, while she thought about how much she missed the peacefulness of looking over cultivated fields from her mother's front stoep where her brother, Harry, bred pigeons.

The pigeons were imprisoned behind chicken wire in small brick nests high above the ground. That was how she felt, like a pigeon, sitting in front of the window in her dingy flat on the third floor of a tall building in Hillbrow; another block of flats obscuring her view.

Only when she leaned out of the window, craning her neck to look up, could she see the sliver of grey sky separating the two buildings.

Anna had not made a single friend in the city after six long months, and was tempted to go home, but she knew that she would not be able to endure the pity, the endless whispering. Above all she could not risk meeting André with his new bride on his arm. How could she have believed him when he said he loved her?

But he should see her now. She ran her fingers through her short, curly hair. She had changed. She no longer wore long skirts and frilly blouses. She had bleached her hair, and had changed her name to

Anne on the advice of a typist working with her in the office. This co-worker had also arranged her only outing to date, which had turned sour when the young man became too goatish; an uneasy experience.

There was a sudden noise. Her eyes lost their glazed look as she came back to the present and realised that a woman had raised her voice. She looked through the window, saw a burly young man holding a woman by her hand, trying to kiss her. She tried to tug free but he was too strong.

Why didn't anybody help her? Surely someone should help. At home everybody helped each other and this would never happen in the middle of the street, Anna thought, as her eyes searched the immediate area, which seemed desolate.

Cars were roaring past while the shouting turned into tears. The woman knelt in front of her admirer, pleading, her red dress torn from one shoulder.

The people in the cars had to see what's happening. But they didn't stop; they were like remote-controlled toy cars on a racetrack.

She noticed a tall, middle-aged man approaching. Her hope surged, but when he reached the scene he hesitated briefly then rushed past, his head retracted into the folds of his brown coat. The coward. Why, maybe she will go down herself!

She hesitated at the door. Wasn't it dangerous? Would the man not turn on her instead? What should she do? Call the police? But what if she had to go to court, or worse still, have to identify the suspect? If set free he could come after her.

The unknown woman had started screaming. Anna licked her dry lips, rubbed her damp palms against her skirt and was transported back to being on stage during a school concert; her heart thudding, and her legs wobbly. Stepping out there would focus attention on her, a shy girl, and she didn't know how the burly man would react.

She had a new thought. What if he knew the woman? Maybe she was a prostitute and he her husband. She was reluctant to intrude; in the platteland it was admissible, but here…

The screaming started afresh, this time on a higher note. It did not sound human at all. Then it ceased. She was drawn to the window, and saw the woman running barefoot down the pavement, free.

The man sprinted after her, his jacket swinging from side to side. Anna opened the window to yell at him to stop. Glancing at the opposite building she saw at least ten faces staring down passively.

EYE OF A NEEDLE

"It's easier to push a camel through the eye of a needle than it is for an older female to get respect.

"You won't know, of course, because you're in this luscious garden with its beautiful flowers and fruit trees. I say children are supposed to be seen and not heard. And here was this child yapping the whole time, not giving me a word in edgewise. What is the world coming to, I ask you, in these modren times? In my day, my mother would've taken me on her knee and slapped my tail."

She had not seen her friend for a while. They had both retired and she, an old snake, had moved to another place. On a visit home to see her mother, she had dropped by.

"You wouldn't believe what I saw," she continued. "My friend introduced me to her grandson, a cute enough boy of about three years. His name was Oedipus. His father's name was probably Oedi and his mother's name Pusina. And they combined them into one of those strange names that people like to make up here in South Africa. Like Patwell, which is a mixture of Patricia and Wellington. Or Dericia, whatever that stands for. Oedipus. Have you ever heard of such a name?

"When I said 'hallo little boy', he frowned, and I thought, uh-oh, what's going on here? A modren baby. No manners and full of frowns and fiemies. She offered me something to eat and I curled myself up to have a good conversation to catch up. But, I couldn't get a word in. This child kept talking all the time.

"And when she made tea she forgot to give me a cup, saucer and a teaspoon. And to put it on a tray. With a little cloth on it. She gave me tea in a mug. A mug, I tell you, with a teaspoon standing up in it, ready to take out my eye. Ai tog, what's this world coming to? Must be that child that's making her kenz before her time.

"She didn't apologise. If she had said 'Angelina, please forgive me, this child is driving me mad', I would've understood. I'm not an unreasonable person. But she didn't apologise, and I was sad.

"To cap it all, she wasn't dressed and wearing stockings. She had this pink-check overall on, slippers and men's socks! As if she had given up or had one foot in the grave. We are only in our seventies. Ai, life had swallowed her up.

"You must understand where I'm coming from, why I couldn't understand. My friend used to be a fearsome teacher in her day. Her grade one class knew who's who and what's what. And here this child was carrying on.

"He wouldn't shut up. 'Ouma, I'm hungry. Ouma, I have to go to the toilet.' She couldn't lie down for five minutes then it was Ouma this and Ouma that. What happened to children out of the water and mouse droppings out of the pepper? I was ready to slap his tail. We were such good friends, her and me. She was human and I was a snake but you would never say. It was almost like we were the same race. And here this brat was giving her the run-around. That's not all. While I was there, this child kept saying my friend must go and make food. On and on he went.

"Just before I left, I wanted to go to the loo. You know how it is with us older ladies who've had a few babies sleeping on our bladders. The toilet was here, next to the main sleeping place. When I came out, there was her daughter-in-law, Eve, whispering into Oedi's ears.

"At first I thought the mother was telling him a secret. That's probably not unusual these days with these modren mummies and modren babies; the mother whispering, telling them they are clever, and then they become clever. We just used to read to them, to teach them a vocabulary. Now they listen to music while they're still in the mother's tummy, and when they come out they can rap. All that nonsense wouldn't have happened in my day, but these are modren times.

"She didn't even greet me properly. If you ask me she's one of those people who show teeth, but in their hearts they say, 'Mog jy vrek'.

"That's why it is said that the world is coming to an end, even before it began. The sky is at the bottom and the ground on top. For example, look at me; do you see these fine lines? Yet someone keeps asking me all the time when I'm getting married again. At my age! I had my husband. I'm not that modren. And all the men dead, and the ones still alive so useless you probably have to put lead in their ears. I don't want a suitcase to carry around.

"I followed this boy back to the sitting place. By this time I was itching to clobber him. When we got there he started on his rag again about my friend who must go and make food now, it was getting late. Then it hit me like a thunderstorm. The mother was sending him. Can you believe that? Eve was controlling my friend through the child. Teaching him to disrespect his own grandmother. Where in the world have you ever seen something like that? It was a sorry sight, I tell you.

"And my poor friend didn't want to face the loneliness of living alone, so she put up with it. She was so embarrassed that I had to witness it. I could tell. I'm psychic, all of us are. Like I said, a camel can pass through the eye of a needle before an older female gets any respect.

"That's why I live alone. I don't want to listen to people complaining about their expensive flower carpets. Then, before you know it, you're put into an old-age hole against your will, and you don't know what happened to all your clothes and your furniture. No, I want to live alone.

"I keep myself busy. I go to the old-age club on Tuesdays. Last year we went to the sea. I brought bottles of sea water for everybody in our street. Usually I'm the one to ask others to bring for me, but this time I fetched it from the sea. I have a picture of myself in a swimming cap. I keep it in my bag. Look here."

She showed a photograph. Curled up, her head sideways like a model.

"I want to live alone. I pray that my children won't decide to move in with me to protect me from burglars and take over my house. Relegating me to sit on a sand heap and watch the world use up time."

THE LIST

He comes home tired, red. He doesn't eat as usual. He sleeps. Questions start pouring into her mind. Why is he so red? Where did he eat? Why is he tired? But she knows, knows that he is sleeping with someone else. A gut feeling that gnaws at her stomach doesn't need the proof of a panty in his pocket or in the wash.

Which raises another question; what to do about it? Does she stay or does she leave? And another; how did they get here? The one moment they were happy, or so she'd thought, and the next he was gone, folded in on himself.

She didn't notice it at first, blamed herself for his lapses in attention, as women tend to do, for his unexplained outbursts, his anger.

To do
Groceries
Bread
Milk
Cheese
The cookies he likes
Chores
Iron shirts
Wash his car

Clean out the garage
Plant marigolds
Pros
Freedom from pain and worry
No humiliation
Not feeling as if she's letting herself down
Cons

Fears
Her friend's son had a breakdown after the divorce
Her cousin's daughter is on antidepressants after learn-
ing about the infidelity of her father
Plans...
Plans...
Does she have to choose between her dignity and the
sanity of her children?

PATCHWORK

Seeking answers

What was required of her? Feeding the baby, washing nappies, cooking and cleaning, taking the older one to school, supervising homework? Was it possible to do all this and get through the day without much effort or feeling? Did she see her twin sister Mira looking at him with an unmistakable invitation after a few drinks? Did she see him noticing, flattered and interested, doing a jig although he never danced? Should she ask him about it? Would he admit it because he always said no? She knew he lied, but could she trust her own eyes?

She was tired of crying, had cried so much already. But although she was unhappy, she still patched up her marriage. Duty, done; self, denied.

Saying no

Last night she dreamt that he was chasing her. She tried to squeeze through the window while he rattled the door, but she couldn't because she had gained so much weight.

This morning she overate again. Her stomach bloated, she felt ill. Yet she crammed more food into her mouth.

If only she had money to buy a house. She lived in a corrugated iron shack. When it rained, the wind blew up the edges of the second-hand aluminium sheets on the roof. It rolled away the boulders holding the roof down. Holes had formed, which required all her bowls and buckets on the dung floor during the rains.

Other men climbed up on ladders to rearrange their roofs. He never did. One hole let through the sky, a boulder obscuring one end. It sagged down, dangerously. She asked him to fix it, but he didn't. He said no.

Her house was falling down, but her smile didn't falter. Occasionally it cracked, but it didn't fade. If she left, where would she go?

Then the boulder fell through the roof. He moved in his sleep, continued snoring.

No, she said.

Mr and Mrs

Domestic chickens
Pecking out an eye
For an eye
Picking at relationships
Bone of conflict
Pecking
Always pecking
And patching

The other woman

What was the question again? Yes, he had an affair; not with her sister, but with a neighbour.

Brought up to consider others, she had tried to be a good person, putting everyone's needs ahead of her own. Now she had lost her kindness. This caused a greater pain than his infidelity.

TO DIE FOR

There was a picture on the wall: three stone-coloured umbrellas of different sizes spread out under each other. God's umbrella was uppermost, the largest, to protect and encompass all. Underneath Him, was a slightly smaller umbrella, signifying the position of the husband. If you blinked it was the same size as the first. Under both was the smallest; the place of women and children.

These umbrellas protected against the drops of rain that represented Satan. They were a sacred image of the divine order.

Her blood spatter was next to the picture. The impact of her head against the wall had broken the skin, causing blood to fly. Headbutted, her nose was bleeding, her lip too. Their dance, which had started in the kitchen, had moved to the lounge.

How did it come to this? She wasn't sure. Married at seventeen to an older man, she had not recognised the war, to marshal her defences. At first it was so subtle that she didn't notice. He didn't like her friends or her family. When they came to visit he became angry. They drifted away. He objected to her going out; she stayed at home. He made her feel guilty about pursuing her interests away from the children.

Invisible bounds ensnared her until she couldn't breathe. When she tried to break them, they were like mist. They're only in your mind, her husband assured her.

He playfully kicked her ankles, elbowed her in her sleep under the guise of turning. A particularly hard blow to her chest left a blue mark for months. It couldn't be talked about, even to her family. It had happened in the dark and didn't exist.

Naïve and eager to please, she couldn't fathom that someone big and strong who loved her could hurt her intentionally. She remained vulnerable, wavering between happy and sad; a see-saw that kept her off balance with the vague sensation that something was wrong.

II

She had been with him long enough to realise that his love lasted as long as his sexual passion. He blamed her for everything. She did not take care of herself, her skin was not supple enough, she had become older. His only option was to get a younger wife.

III

An older woman becomes difficult. As soon as she sees her true place she starts to rebel. A younger model is needed then, one that still has stars in her eyes and believes in the dream of love as beautiful and everlasting; one that can be bombarded with love acts while her subjugation is set in motion.

However, breaking down a new woman takes time. And to start again is hard work; not lightly undertaken at an advanced age. Better to stay with the one into whom he's already put all the labour. He had broken her down once and could do it again. She just needed a sterner hand.

But he wanted a new sexual partner and she would just have to accept that. He was a man after all, with needs. He had rights, he announced to his group of friends. There was general agreement.

They were at someone's house drinking, laughing and telling tall stories; building solidarity, discussing women.

"And if she doesn't want to agree, you make her," a friend asserted.

Laughter. They all chipped in.

"I have a stick named Jimmy especially for my wife."

"Nay, man, I just slap her. And when you've done it once or twice, you just lift your hand and she pisses her pants."

"Yes, beat in the love." A boxing gesture.

"You have to slap your daughters too, when they're young, to make it easier for their future husbands."

"Then you give their brothers permission to slap them. They need practice."

"Listen here, this is the best: tell your son from a young age that women are stupid."

"That they're just good for one thing."

"Which reminds me, when I get home now there's going to be trouble."

"What're you going to do, Boetie?"

"I'm going to shake that woman awake and demand sex."

"What? You wouldn't."

"Just watch me. Me, I rape."

There was laughter and encouragement as he left to carry out his threat. He was whistling when he opened the back door.

He had just touched her, when she jumped up, locked herself in the bathroom. He was livid. After he had already promised his mates; this was an affront. A man denied access to a woman he regarded as his property, he developed acute hostility. He withheld money and slept hugging himself, curled away from her; a frown in repose.

IV

That was when the abuse started.

He slammed her wrist against the wall, breaking it. She sank down onto her knees. He yanked her up by her arm, pulling her shoulder almost out of joint. She fell. He kicked her head, her chest. She curled into a foetal ball, her hands covering her head.

She pretended to be unconscious on the floor, a strategy to make him stop and start on his crying apologies; the next stage after a beating. It worked. He brought her flowers and chocolates. He promised never to do it again. She believed him.

V

The picture of the umbrellas was her husband's; he had stuck it on the wall when he became saved, discarding his old religion in a traditional church to join the growing movement of fundamentalist Christianity. He had a spare copy on top of his wardrobe.

The umbrellas depicted God's authority. Converts had to live under it or face Satan's rain. Evangelism was sweeping through the land, a revival. The Bible was supreme and the scripture said 'woman submit to your husband'. Even if he assaults you, a good woman should heed this advice. Her only claim to being was through her husband.

Countless women had joined the church. Yet she held out, putting her marriage and the spiritual lives of her three children in peril.

It had been hard to oppose. Birds of a feather flocked together and none flocked so hard like the adherents of the new faith. She was an outcast.

A woman had to be quiet, gentle, a 'prayer warrior' whose prayers would move mountains.

VI

He and his friends were discussing television.

"What's your favourite series, bru?"

"There's so much to pick from. Vikings, the Vatican, fighting over thrones."

"Ja, at last they are catering for real men." The boxer hit the table as he said 'real men', two thumps.

"Not all this sissy stuff that they had previously."

"Things were better in the past. Men went to war and women stayed at home."

"They knew their place. They made themselves pretty for the man's return."

"Did you see, in the one about the Vatican, one man slept with his sister?"

Hoots of laughter.

"Did you see the one where this oke traded his sister for an army?"

"Those were the good old days."

VII

She felt uneasy when he watched these television programmes. Most men in her life were uncomfortable with women trying to advance, and wanted to reinstate the past.

So many Hollywood series had appeared with on-screen violence against women. On the one about Blackbeard, British soldiers beat up a young girl and buried her alive.

Afraid the television programmes would give him more ideas on how to increase her torment, on the days he watched she tiptoed around to please him. It ignited her fear.

There seemed to be an intense war against women, which nobody noticed. Their only use was to provide sex; preferably on their knees, being taken from behind.

VIII

Her daughter had married recently, to a man whose brother had founded a church. As the lead pastor, he conducted the wedding and interpreted the picture of the umbrellas. The husband, as the head of the house, prayed directly to God. The wife looked up to and respected the husband, because through him she could reach God; there was no direct line. Stepping out from under the umbrella of God's authority meant inviting Satan.

She was appalled. Morality and a set of principles had become obsolete. All that was required was to fall on one's knees and pray to be forgiven. Replicating the same sin was alright because the crying and the praying could be repeated as needed, like Panado or an antidiarrhoeal tablet.

She couldn't sleep at night, worrying about her daughter. Her life would be one of submission with no earthly reward. She couldn't warn her because she had been moved into the position of the mother-in-law, long disarmed by ridicule. And her experience and the knowledge gained from thirty-eight years of marriage could not be passed on; she was ashamed. How do you speak the unspeakable?

IX

There was a bruise on her daughter's arm, which was explained away as bumping into the wardrobe. The realisation that her daughter may be abused hurt more than any kick on the ankle. It seared her mind. Would her second daughter fall into the same abyss if she shirked her duty?

She removed the umbrellas from the wall when her husband went away for a week to a church conference. She tore it into strips, stomped on it, and threw it into the dustbin. She replaced it with the wheel of power and control she had found on the internet.

The wheel set down the tactics men had learned on how to dominate and control a spouse. These were passed from one generation to the next. The spokes of the wheel were coercion, threats, intimidation, emotional abuse, isolation and economic abuse, male privilege, using children, minimisation, denying and blame. Physical and sexual violence formed the outer rim.

These tactics were universal, the lived experience of most battered women, and were reinforced through social, cultural and institutional means.

X

She had been conditioned to accept. She was used to being ignored, used to being treated badly. She had built up a secret way of coping. First was to create distance between the violence and her feelings about it. Don't think about it and soon it will disappear. Only that exists which you allow to exist. It had always served her well.

But spurred by the courageous act of removing the umbrellas, concern for her daughter, and her husband's infidelity – a thorn in the flesh for a long time – she called her husband and announced that she wanted a divorce.

XI

When he came home, he saw that the picture had been moved. Threatening divorce plus moving his property; that was too much for any man to bear. Without a word he removed her picture, went to retrieve his spare one, and replaced it on the wall. The wheel he flung onto a chair.

A man who couldn't control his woman, causing the other men to shake their heads in disgust? The thought inflamed his rage.

He approached her where she was standing in front of the stove to warm his food. He grabbed her neck and slammed her against the wall. Her head knocked back and bounced forward. She clawed at his hand. This infuriated him. He put both hands around her neck. She started to choke, turn blue. Fear released her bladder.

The silence made it surreal. If it was accompanied by shouting and screaming, hers or his, it would make a dent in the universe, but the silence made it dreamlike, intimate. His snarl and the hatred in his eyes were therefore a mistake. She couldn't believe that it was happening, again; he had promised. Her body felt numb.

Their private dance took them across the room a few times, he leading, she stumbling, her ragdoll body following without protest. Blood in her mouth; she had bitten her tongue. But the children would not be disturbed in their sleep.

"I'm going to kill you, you fuckin' bitch."

The words exploded into the silence, breaking the spell, galvanising her into action. She began to fight for the right to live. Locked in a deadly dance with her devil, she pushed him with her sound arm, kneed him in the groin. He fell.

She gasped for air, trying to clear her head. Her safety plan. Where did she put the car keys, the bag with her identity card, money, credit card and a change of clothes? She couldn't remember.

Although she had prepared for it, she never thought that she would actually leave. She had read about a safety plan in her research into surviving an abusive relationship. She had thought about it a lot, done little.

She ran, crawled under the bed. He pulled her out by her legs, turned her over. She saw the knife in his hand. Concern for her children forgotten, she uttered a primal scream which echoed through the house.

"Shut up, you witch." He sat on her chest, stabbed her twice.

The neighbour heard her scream, knocked on the window, saw him sitting on her chest. Alarmed at being discovered – he was going to blame a burglar – he slashed his own throat superficially, nicking his voice box.

While waiting for the ambulance it gave her no joy to watch him injured, unable to speak, blood slowly seeping from his neck. The bitter taste of hatred settled on her tongue. She fastened her eyes on the picture that had replaced the umbrellas, which had slid onto the floor. Two pairs of legs, her daughters; they were looking at the wheel.

She regretted screaming, waking them and her son. Where was her son? Fifteen, he was kneeling next to his father, glaring at her. She started crying.

"It's delayed shock," the neighbour said, a tall, thin woman. "Bring some sugar water. Please stop, dearie. You're making yourself sick. The ambulance is on the way."

Shuddering, gasping sobs. She lost the tears of all mothers when they realised that, in spite of their teaching and influence, they had raised sons who were like the fathers; that under the tutelage of the patriarchs, their sons had grown up to disrespect women. Her physical pain had receded, overtaken by mental and emotional agony. She cried and cried.

"Please don't cry, Mummy." Her daughters were on their knees, crying with her.

XII

She had been discharged from hospital and was cleaning her bedroom. Her husband was going to kill her. She knew it with a certainty that stuck to her bones.

He was also home, but was hardly speaking to her, casting brooding glances of such malice that it made his eyes squint. He would kill her, and the choice she had to make was whether to wait for it or get out. But that meant leaving everything behind; her children, her friends, her rose garden, her specially fitted kitchen, a lifetime of accumulated possessions; they belonged to her because she had found them and arranged them to the best *feng shui*.

Stay or leave, even if it was just emotionally, to lessen the pain of being abused. She shook the dust out of a small rug. She couldn't allow him to know, though. He wasn't a man who would relish being left by a woman. He was too proud.

But maybe this time he would change after seeing how much he hurt her. Her hands became still. Having married straight after her matric examination, she had never worked. With no skills and no confidence, she was afraid. She changed the duvet cover. Dust particles shivered in a ray of sun.

GLOSSARY

Model C school – multiracial school with better facilities
Moerkoffie – homebrewed coffee
Chommies – friends
Group Areas Act and Population Registration Act – apartheid laws restricting where people could live by classifying them into different racial groups.
Tik – crystal meth
Braai – barbeque
Toyi-toying – a war dance
Drinking song – Morning uncle, morning aunt, where's Sannie. She went for water at the dam. Her dress has a tear. The young men look through it.
Hi-fi – music system
Biltong – beef jerky
Koeksister – local doughnut
Lekker vat en sit – living together
Geen baster mag in die vergadering van die Here kom nie – No mixed breed may enter the community of God
Knobkierie – walking stick

Platteland – rural area
Modren – a mispronunciation of modern
Fiemies – nonsense
Kenz – senile
Mog jy vrek – may you die

ABOUT THE AUTHOR

 Cornelia Smith Fick (Connie Fick) was born in Grasmere, a small settlement south of Johannesburg, during apartheid. The second daughter of an Anglican priest and a garment worker, she excelled at the local secondary school where, in her spare time, she wrote songs and painted portraits. Her fondest memory of this school is reciting the rhyme of a shoe maker, 'Koen waar is my skoen', in the yearly concert, wearing her grade one teacher's high heels and handbag.

She was longlisted for the Sol Plaatje EU Poetry Award in 2016 and has just published an ebook, Eye of a Needle, which originated as a thesis for the Masters in Creative Writing at Rhodes University. A nurse by profession, she worked for a number of years as the editor of Health & Hygiene, a monthly primary health care magazine. She was a freelance writer for Takalani Sesame (radio and TV). Her poems and short stories have been published in local and international literary magazines and anthologies eg. Itch, Botsotso, Experimental Writing: Volume 1, Africa VS Latin America, Ladyboxbooks.com and Atlanta Review. She lives in Johannesburg with her family and two dogs.

www.ingramcontent.com/pod-product-compliance
Lightning Source LLC
Chambersburg PA
CBHW021042130626
46552CB00005B/1982